I0677880

ONLY WHEN THEY'RE LITTLE

The Story Of An Appalachian Family

ONLY WHEN THEY'RE LITTLE

The Story Of An Appalachian Family

By KATE PICKENS DAY

Illustrated by Margaret Pickens

Edited, with an introduction by
Nancy Carol Joyner

APPALACHIAN CONSORTIUM PRESS
Boone, North Carolina

The Appalachian Consortium was a non-profit educational organization composed of institutions and agencies located in Southern Appalachia. From 1973 to 2004, its members published pioneering works in Appalachian studies documenting the history and cultural heritage of the region. The Appalachian Consortium Press was the first publisher devoted solely to the region and many of the works it published remain seminal in the field to this day.

With funding from the Andrew W. Mellon Foundation and the National Endowment for the Humanities through the Humanities Open Book Program, Appalachian State University has published new paperback and open access digital editions of works from the Appalachian Consortium Press.

www.collections.library.appstate.edu/appconsortiumbooks

This work is licensed under a Creative Commons BY-NC-ND license. To view a copy of the license, visit http://creativecommons.org/licenses.

Original copyright © 1985 by the Appalachian Consortium Press.

ISBN (pbk.: alk. Paper): 978-1-4696-3816-4
ISBN (ebook): 978-1-4696-3818-8

Distributed by the University of North Carolina Press
www.uncpress.org

Introduction

Only When They're Little is a story set in the mountains, but it is no tall tale. It is the fictional account of an actual family whose Scotch-Irish ancestors immigrated to western North Carolina in the early nineteenth century. The book begins in 1904, when the Barker family undertakes the elaborate move of twenty miles across the mountain to "Tarpley," a small town a few miles north of Asheville. It concludes nearly a half century later, in the late forties. Thus it describes the situation and relates significant events in the life of an Appalachian family during the first half of the twentieth century.

The family consists of Cora and Joe Barker and their eight children. Joe, a farmer/blacksmith/carpenter, is presented as a stabilizing force in spite of his bewilderment at the sweeping economic changes within the area. Cora, the dynamic center of the book, is portrayed as a energetic, ambitious woman who is devoted to her family and determined that they succeed. The eight children, with varying abilities and interests, appear as a relatively close-knit group who absorb almost unquestioningly their parents' attitudes and value system. As middle-income white Protestants with an orientation toward education and upward mobility, they are typical of thousands of families living in the southern highlands.

For the past hundred years residents of southern Appalachia have been stereotyped as eccentric, ignorant recluses whose principal occupation is to protect the family still from the "revenoors." Families are presented as male-dominated, ultra-conservative, and clannish in the extreme. The creators of the comic strips "Li'l Abner" and "Snuffy Smith" and the producers of such television programs as "Hee Haw" and "The Dukes of Hazzard" have done much to perpetuate such a myth, but serious studies have also encouraged the view that mountain people are distinct from "mainstream" America partially because of their low income and inadequate education.

This book helps to amend the view of the "oddity" of mountain people by providing a portrait of a family similar in many ways to members of the middle class anywhere in the United States. At the same time it maintains an awareness of the area and the definite effect of the region on the lives of the people. It emphasizes for example the closeness of the southern Appalachian family, a theme often

i

mentioned in studies characterizing the area. The author also emphasizes the importance of education for the mountain people and the impetus for personal achievement, themes often overlooked. Another significant aspect of the book is the portrayal of Appalachian women as intelligent, independent, and assertive.

In a 1981 interview the author was asked if she regarded her life in an Appalachian community as being more difficult than if she had lived elsewhere. This was her reply:

> During my early life it was a poor community compared to today's standards, but it was not to the point where people had to really suffer for things. If you were willing to work, and tried, you could have a comfortable and decent home and a decent home life. And while education wasn't on every corner and it wasn't up to the point where it got to be later, we didn't *have* to be ignorant, and there were plenty who never were. My mother was able to teach school, and so was my grandmother. And as for the values of life and for her attitude toward it, I think that the mountain woman would stack up with any other.

The story of the Barker family, especially that of Cora Barker, encourages a re-evaluation of attitudes about life in the southern highlands in the twentieth century.

The author was born Esther Katharine Pickens in Weaverville, North Carolina, on February 20, 1894. Three years later she moved with her family to Swannanoa, twenty miles away, but in 1904 they returned to Weaverville, primarily in order to afford schooling for the children at Weaver College. She, along with five of her seven brothers and sisters, completed the academic program there. After her graduation in 1913, she taught in public schools until her marriage in 1918 to Ben T. Day, the owner of a lumber company in Easley, South Carolina. The house they built in 1920 was her home until her death in 1984. She was the mother of two, grandmother of five, and great grandmother of seven.

Although raising her two daughters and a niece was her principal occupation during her married life, Kate Pickens Day had many interests beyond her family. She helped to organize and was first president of the Woman's Club of Easley and was active in many other civic organizations; she held many positions of responsibility in the Methodist Church; she kept books for her husband's expanding business; she wrote a column for the local weekly newspaper; she raised flowers, vegetables, and chickens; she did a variety of handwork: tatting, knitting, crocheting, and quilting; she painted in oils and water color. After her husband's death in 1949, she traveled widely, making extended trips to unfamiliar areas in this country as well as to Mexico and Europe. She also gave art lessons in her home in Easley and worked for several years as a bookkeeper in a law office in Asheville. In 1951 she published privately an extensive genealogy, *The Pickens Family*.

Her life was an exceptionally active one until, in 1974, her eyesight began to fail. Two cataract operations resulted in inoperable detached retinas, and with her diminishing ability to see she was deprived of the activities that most absorbed her time—painting, needlework, and gardening. In 1980 her seriously impaired heart forced her permanently to bed.

After eighty-six unstintingly energetic years, her forced physical activity was anathema to her. She couldn't see well enough to read, but she could see well enough to write. Surreptitiously at first, fearing her family might think her "a fool to try such a thing" at her age, she began to write a novel. With the encouragement of her daughters, however, she threw herself wholeheartedly into her project, writing in longhand on the days she had the physical stamina and sufficient sight to do so, sending the pages along to her daughter, Margaret, to type, while her daughter, Esther, cared for her. The result is *Only When They're Little*.

The book combines the genres of autobiography and fiction: it is a memoir told from three points of view. Most prominent is the voice of Cora, a fictionalization of Kate's mother, Clemma Ozora, remembering the difficulties and delights of raising eight children. Occasionally the point of view switches to Jane, the fictional character who most closely resembles Kate. A third voice is that of the author herself as she speaks reflectively, commenting on the changes she has observed over fifty years. Sometimes she does so in humorous dismay, sometimes in indignation, but always with perception and sincerity. The book does not preach, but it does convey strong opinions.

As Huckleberry Finn says about the book Mr. Mark Twain wrote about Tom Sawyer, this one also contains some "stretchers." The events in the book do not represent a factual account of the author's family. Character and place names are changed; happenings are telescoped, combined, and occasionally fabricated. One poignant example is the story here of Dan, who represents Hugh, the adored youngest brother who died of a heart attack before he was thirty. Kate said she couldn't bear to record that, so she created a new life for him, complete with family, in London. On the other hand, the author makes no attempt to whitewash all the familial experiences that have led to unhappy memories. Although she deliberately avoids factual accuracy, she confronts the truth head-on. It is a truer book than a mere factual account could make it. I know. I am the niece she raised.

Happily, the author's relatives have made this book a real family project. Kate's daughters, Margaret Day Ball of Wayne, Illinois, and Esther Day Moore, of Easley, South Carolina, have provided material assistance by typing the manuscript, proof reading the typescript, and encouraging in other ways the completion of the work. I have edited the typescript, making minor revisions by occasionally re-ordering paragraphs, avoiding repetitions, and smoothing out inconsistencies. In every case, however, I have attempted to keep intact the individual quality of the author's style. The illustrations have been generously provided by Kate's younger sister, Margaret Pickens of Weaverville, North Carolina. She has based her drawing on the events recorded and on her own memories, and when possible she has used as models photographs of family members. The author once said in an interview, "Not any of us ought to be parasites. We all ought to contribute something to the world—that's what we're here for." With gratitude and devotion, members of Kate Pickens Day's family have added their contributions to the author's larger one in creating *Only When They're Little.*

Nancy Carol Joyner
Western Carolina University

1

"Jane! Ring the bell! Then make haste and run on down to the spring house and get the milk and butter! Hurry now!" Cora's voice was tense and strident.

Obediently Jane set down the bowl of tomatoes she had just sliced, went hurriedly through the dismantled kitchen, took the old-fashioned hand bell from the water shelf on the back porch, and shook it vigorously up and down. Replacing the bell, she raced across the porch, down the steps, and on to the spring path.

Cora watched her ten-year-old daughter disappear around the bend of the path and thought that this must be the most confusing day in Jane's life. Probably she was completely bewildered by all the unfamiliar things that were happening in this very familiar place.

Joe and Cora Barker had lived in the little valley bordering the Swannanoa River for fifteen years. More than that, Joe had lived his life in the house they were preparing to leave. When his father died in 1890, Joe had inherited the homestead and about a hundred acres of land. With his brother John, he had "kept batch" as they called it. There was a highway running through one side of the farm, known to local settlers as the Big Road, and Joe and John had a blacksmith shop bordering the road. Old Uncle Bill, who had been the general handyman about the place for as long as anyone could remember, lived in a cabin behind the main house.

Cora Graham had been a plump little girl with bright dark eyes and hair that inclined to curl. In a family of five children she was the odd one—somehow the others formed two pairs and Cora from the beginning had learned to play by herself. She had lived in an imaginary world peopled by her dolls who, according to her, were an ideal group of brothers and sisters who never quarreled and who were completely loyal to each other and made a very special family.

One day when old Aunt Betsy was at the Graham house to do the week's laundering, Cora dwelt at length to her on the virtues of her family. Finally Betsy shook her head. "Humph—humph, Miss Cora," she said. "Peoples don't live like dat. When dey grows up de chillun lots o' times don' even lak each udder. Dey quarrel and sometimes dey fights. Dey moves away from each udder when dey grows up and dat's de last of 'em. Families just don' be lak yours when dey grows up. No, sir, just only when dey's little."

Naturally, Cora didn't believe Aunt Betsy. She was sure she knew what kind of family hers would be and that they wouldn't be the way she wanted them to be only when they were little, so she went on with her dreaming and planning.

When Cora finished her teacher training and came to take charge of the one-teacher school in Swannanoa, she felt ready to begin raising a family. Joe Barker had also begun to look for a helpmate, and soon after they met they decided to marry at the end of the school term. After the wedding and a short honeymoon, Cora moved into the Barker home and took over the housekeeping. Uncle Bill was her salvation. He did the milking, helped her with the kitchen garden, and taught her how to care for the chickens, turkeys, and guineas. He showed her how to make butter, dry apples, and "leather breeches" beans. In fact, she wondered how she ever got to be nineteen years old and know so little.

Life on the farm for the most part was placid and agreeable, the biggest changes occurring when every other year a new member was added to the Barker household. Their first child was a daughter, Mary, and two years later Nathan was born. Then came Jane, Janice, Robert, Millie, and Susan. Once when Cora's waspish-tongued aunt had been visiting, she told folks back home, "Poor Cora, she never gets one baby off her lap until there's another one to go on it!" Having seven children in fifteen years proved the aunt right, but Cora did not think of herself as poor. She had the family she had wanted ever since she was a little girl.

When Mary began to talk and could say "Papa" and "Mama," almost unconsciously Joe and Cora adopted Mary's dialect. Soon they became not "Joe" and "Cora" but "Papa" and "Mama" to each other.

Papa was well content with his life. He enjoyed his big family and worked hard in his blacksmith shop on the farm. He had no desire to make a change, but Mama did. Sometimes Mama's restlessness worried him and he grew peevish. "Why can't the kids grow up here?" he asked her. "I've never lived anywhere else and I've got along all right."

"But Joe, times are changing," Mama would answer. "The children must get an education. They can't help themselves if we don't give them a chance, and we can't afford to send them off to school. Now, if we moved to Tarpley, we could see to it that they have an education."

For several weeks the discussion had gone on. Papa didn't think Mama really knew what she was talking about when she predicted that automobiles and hard surfaced roads would bring so many changes. And he could not visualize the decline of a blacksmith shop or the lessening need for horses and farm tools and equipment. However, in the end he capitulated and the farm was sold.

Mama herself had some misgivings about the move. She realized that Papa was making a real sacrifice by agreeing to sell and that it would be hard for a person to leave the only house he had ever known. But she was deeply convinced that the children must have a better opportunity than this community could give them. Mama was herself a native mountaineer just as Papa was, but neither of them belonged to the shiftless, illiterate type that modern novelists like to portray as typical mountain people. In spite of lack of transportation and difficulty in communication, they were able to acquire some

3

education, to have access to books, to travel a bit, and to see each generation advance a little. Poor they might be, but by hard work and frugal habits they could live comfortably.

Tarpley was a little town about twenty miles away, where a struggling small college was located. It had a preparatory department where students could "fill in the gaps" left because of inadequate elementary and high school training. Mama had it all figured out. By living in Tarpley, all her children could attend as day students and have only tuition to pay. She was willing to make any sacrifice that might be required of her to get them all through school.

Mama and Papa set the date on their calendar for the big move. It was June 17, 1904. Finally, the day had arrived.

2

The ringing of the dinner bell speedily assembled the members of the family. They came into the ghost-like house, with its curtainless windows and bare rooms that echoed their footsteps, and were silenced by the strangeness of it all. Papa and Uncle John came from the shop across the way. Nathan and Bob, aged twelve and six, had been picking the last of the cornfield beans with old Uncle Bob. Janice, eight years old, had been minding the two youngest children, three-year-old Millie and Susan, just four months old. Fourteen-year-old Mary, the oldest child, and Jane, aged ten, helped to put the food on the big, round, claw-footed oak table. Even though most of the furniture had been packed, the kitchen furnishings were still usable, and the family as usual sat down together for their breakfast. Healthy appetites helped make the ham biscuits, sliced tomatoes, applesauce, and gingerbread disappear in a hurry. In a few minutes the loading resumed.

The railway ran in sight of the farm in Swannanoa but did not go to Tarpley, so the only way to transport themselves was by horse-drawn vehicles. A huge wagon with high boarded sides was backed up to the door and the tailgate was let down. It soon began to bulge with its cargo of wooden beds, straw mattresses, feather beds, the parlor sofa, the Estey organ, bureaus, chests, tables, chairs, and a hodgepodge of household goods. Neighborly cousin Bert was driving this wagon with Mary sitting up front next to him because she had visited relatives in Tarpley and knew the way.

Nathan, called Nate, would drive the top buggy and Mama would ride with him holding Susan on her lap, while Millie sat between them. Jane, Janice, and Bob were left to go with Papa, who would drive the two-horse farm wagon. Janice had claimed the wagon seat with Papa, so Jane would have Bob for company in the back of the jolting wagon, which was going to make for a tedious and uncomfortable ride. The wagon bed was filled with odds and ends that the larger wagon could not take and articles that had been overlooked until the last minute.

Off they started on their twenty-mile trek, cousin Bert in front, Nate in the middle, and Papa bringing up the rear. Soon Bob became restless sitting in the wagon. In his wriggling around he discovered the almost forgotten wooden churn which had been added at the last minute. It appealed to him as a good place to sit "high" and see things. Promptly he crawled up on top of it and things went smoothly for a time, but as the wagon rounded the curve on a downhill grade, the churn, top heavy with its burden, turned over on its side, catapulting Bob across the wagon. His head struck a standard and cut a gash in his forehead. By some good fortune they were passing by a watering trough just off the roadside. It was a big log hollowed out like a canoe and was fed fresh water continuously from a pipeline connected with a spring on the hill above the road. It was in a shady spot, and because of the dampness, ferns and other green plants grew in profusion around it. Papa stopped the wagon, washed the grime from his bleeding offspring, and gave the horses a drink.

Soon after the churn episode Bob burrowed into a corner of the wagon and went to sleep. Jane had an old, braided rug folded up for a seat. It was wedged between a box of dishes and some old pots and pans. Relieved of having to watch after Bob for the moment, she let her thoughts dwell on the confusion and panic she had felt all day. Why, she asked herself, was a one-teacher school so bad? She had been happy in hers and was sure she had learned lots of things. This year the teacher had let her help with spelling and writing lessons for the smaller children and she had loved doing it. She hadn't minded

taking her turn at sweeping the floors or cleaning the blackboards either, and as for germs being so deadly, didn't all of them at home drink from the same gourd dipper hanging by the spring? And why was Uncle Bill not coming to Tarpley to live with them? Jane had followed him around ever since she was a toddler and he seemed as near to her as her own parents. Who would help him hunt the guineas' nests now or who would go with him to the woods to hunt chestnuts and chinquapins in the fall, and couldn't she find more wild strawberries in the spring than he could? Since he was not coming to Tarpley, who would do the milking? She was afraid she knew the answer to that.

As the caravan neared Asheville, another crisis occurred. Papa leaped from the wagon and ran to the horses' heads, signaling Nate to do the same. They held on to their bridles and spoke soothingly to the horses just as the object of their concern went chugging by, "making at least twenty-five miles an hour," Papa said. Jane was startled out of her reverie and stared goggle-eyed as the automobile went out of sight. She had never seen one before. "My goodness," she said to Bob. "Didn't it look just like a buggy running along without a horse!"

Drivers were beginning to expect such interruptions in their traveling. The horses showed antagonism and fear for these noisy machines and many farmers resented the automobile for the trouble it caused. When the Oldsmobile chugged by, Papa had trouble enough with his horses. Gentle old Prince only rolled his eyes and stamped his feet a bit, but Dixie and Dell, both young and skittish, tried to bolt. It took all Papa's strength to keep them from running away.

Concentrating her attention on the horses, Jane remembered the time when Janice, the musician of the family, was playing songs she had heard by ear. She had played some familiar songs on the organ when she turned to Bob and said, "Listen, Bob, I'll play 'Dixie' for you." When she had finished the song, Bob was delighted. He patted her arm and said, "Now, Janice, play Dell."

As the horses clip-clopped along the street across the square in Asheville, Jane let her gaze wander over the pictures the wagons and their occupants made as they were reflected in the plate glass windows along the way. Already she was homesick for the Swannanoa Valley and all the dear, familiar things she was leaving. She didn't cry but her heart felt lonely and unutterably sad.

7

It was almost dusk when the weary travelers arrived in Tarpley. The house Papa had bought with money from the sale of the farm was no architect's dream. It was very plain with no gingerbread trimming or ornamental woodwork of any kind. Shaped like a big square box, it had four rooms downstairs and four on the second floor, with a hallway running through the center of each floor. A wide porch with bannisters ran across the front while a kitchen extension was built back of the dining room with an L-shaped porch on two sides of it. There was no electricity and no plumbing. The well house joined the back porch. Water was drawn by a pulley and chain with a wooden bucket on either end. As one bucket went down into the well the other one came up. Behind the small barn at the back of the house was the outhouse. A fence enclosed the two acres of land in the plot, located in a narrow valley, with hills rising up sharply on two sides. There was nothing fancy about the house or the property, but both would be adequate for the Barker family.

Mama's sister Sally lived in Tarpley, and she met them at the house with a basket of food for supper. That was a wonderful help since the big old kitchen range would have to be connected before they could even have hot water. Beds had to be set up before they could sleep. After the disorder and confusion, when much was accomplished, finally out of sheer exhaustion everyone went to bed.

After two weeks the strange beds began to feel natural. Jane no longer woke in the morning expecting to see the wallpaper of her old room or to hear the train whistle and other familiar sounds of the farm left behind. She and the rest of the Barkers gradually became accustomed to their new home and its surroundings. Jane still missed Swannanoa though and told Mama so. Mama told Jane that she was sure Jane would like Tarpley better as soon as school started.

3

On the Monday morning when schools reopened, Mary (with Mama's coaching) was able to enter Tarpley College as a freshman. Nate was enrolled in the seventh grade, Jane in the fifth, Janice in the third, and Bob in the first. The catapulting of the Barker family into the Tarpley school system made little impact on the school itself, but it certainly put Mama and her brood into a merry-go-round of activity that, as she said, made her dizzy to think about.

Mama said her coat tails never caught up with her that winter. What a scramble it was to outfit and keep five children in school! But that was not all. There were two more children to be cared for and meals to be cooked for a family of nine. Mama wondered, as Jane had, how they would get along without Uncle Bill. Her only help was Aunt Althea, who came on Mondays to do the wash and received

seventy-five cents a day. In the well house was a bench holding three zinc tubs filled with water, and nearby was the big iron pot which the Negro washerwoman also filled with water before she built a fire under it. With a scrub board and homemade lye soap she washed the clothes and then put them in the big pot to boil. Ladling them out of the suds, she put them first in one of the zinc tubs and then the other. Aunt Althea had to wring each article by hand as it was moved from one rinsing tub to the next before it was ready for the clothes line.

At the end of wash day, Aunt Althea left a mountain of unironed clothes to wrestle with. There were starched pieces that had to be sprinkled down—shirts and collars for the men, petticoats and dresses for the girls, pillow cases, centerpieces and other household linens. It all had to be done with a sad iron heated in front of the grate or on top of the kitchen range. Mary, Jane, and even Janice had to take turns almost every afternoon when they came in from school. They were lucky if they completed the job by Saturday before beginning again on Monday. But as the children became adjusted to their schools, they became more involved in outside activities, which meant that Mama got less and less help with the chores.

Reports were sent to parents at the end of a grading period, and Mama was more anxious than the children to get the first reports. Mary's and Janice's work was rated excellent, Jane's was good, Nate's was fair, but he was on the baseball and tennis teams and that meant more to him. Bob's report was poor. Mama found the last report hard to accept, but she finally decided the fault must lie in the teacher.

One afternoon when the group had come in from school, they were seated around the kitchen table having a snack and rehashing the day's experiences. Janice said importantly, "I wrote a poem today."

"Oh," said Mama. "What was the poem about?"

"About families."

"What's a poem?" piped up Bob.

"It's when you write some lines and the words at the end of them sound just alike, but they are not the same words," explained Janice.

"Maybe you would like to read your poem to us," suggested Mama.

So Janice, trying to look very grown-up, got out her notebook. "The name of this poem," she said, "is 'Shall Ever Be.' It goes this way:

I belong to a big family.
Seven and two make nine, you see.
    Shall ever be.

Mary is the oldest of my mother's.
I love her better than thermometers.
    Shall ever be.

Nathan, or Nate, he precipitates.
You can see him standing by the gate.
    Shall ever be.

Jane's name ought to have been Flossie
Because she always has been bossy.
    Shall ever be.

There's two more sisters and a brother,
Who like to fight each with the other.
    Shall ever be."

Nate set down his glass, picked up his cap, and started for the door. He turned and said, "Wouldn't you know it? In this family we've got a poet!" Then he waved to Janice mischievously and called, "Bye, shall ever be!"

There was an open meeting of a literary society into which Mary had been initiated, and the public was invited. Mama thought the Barker family should go, and it never occurred to her that the smaller children would be better left at home. From Papa down to baby Susan they were dressed in their best and, as it had been their custom on the farm, they all rode in the wagon to the college. Upon arrival, they all went in together and sat all in a row on one bench. This arrangement was humiliating to Jane. Around her she saw her friends seated in groups of twos and threes, unencumbered by parents or smaller brothers and sisters. She fervently wished that she didn't have to sit there between Bob and Susan, trying to keep them quiet.

Even Mama realized that her enthusiasm had carried her too far. The fact that the folks in the valley traveled "en famille" to any public occasion did not quite fit in with the Tarpley customs. From now on she and Papa would take turns staying home with the smaller children.

11

She felt almost sure that Papa would rather have stayed home this time.

It was soon evident that school and its activities would interfere with all family routines anyway. There was some special place for Mary to go every afternoon after school, and she was beginning to want to go out at night. Nate's obsession with sports called for daily practice, which in turn interfered with the wood bin. It never got really filled anymore. Mama was lucky if she got Nate to chop enough ahead to keep the fires going a few hours at a time. Some days he was late getting home in time to do the milking, and of course Jane resented having an extra chore.

Bob was also unpredictable. When he failed to turn up at the end of a school day, Jane or Janice was dispatched to find him. Once he couldn't find his cap, and when Jane caught sight of him, he was, she said, "wandering around waiting for his cap to come to him" instead of hunting it. Another day he found a stray kitten and was lugging it home with him. When Jane explained that it probably belonged to someone and he had better let it go, he was reluctant to release it. "It belongs to me now," he argued indignantly, "because I found it, didn't I?"

Bob had a special affection for his cap and wore it constantly, removing it when he came inside the house only when reminded to do so. Soon the boys in his grade discovered his attachment to his

headgear and loved to tease him. One afternoon after school, Janice went out and saw a commotion on the playground. Some boys had snatched Bob's cap and were having a fine time playing catch with it, while Bob ran from one boy to another trying ineffectually to retrieve his property. Janice threw down her book satchel, made for the boy who held the cap, and before he was aware of her nearness, she grabbed him by his red hair and with both hands held on for dear life.

It wasn't an every day occurrence to see a boy and girl fracas on the school grounds. This one was fast and furious, and it was over in a few minutes. Bob's cap was recovered, Janice's dress was torn, her hair ribbon was lost, and there was a scratch down one check, but the redhead had his battle scars too. Fingernail marks were on his face, buttons were ripped off the front of his shirt, and the pain from the hair pulling caused him to go home howling. Bob shamefacedly picked up his cap, dusted it off, and he and Janice walked home in silence.

Mama was disturbed to hear about the fight. She worried for fear there might be an aftermath and probably further troubles because of it. She realized that she had not counted on this kind of trouble when she was planning to put the children in school at Tarpley, but when a week went by and no further mention was made of the fight, she began to breathe easy again.

4

In 1909 Mary was a member of the graduating class of Tarpley College. Her last year at school had been unusually pleasant. There were less than 400 students at the school. Rich people did not send their children to a struggling small college like Tarpley, so the backgrounds of most students were similar and the school atmosphere was unpretentious and friendly. Joe Tolbert, also a senior, had been Mary's escort to a number of school events and they were good friends. Mary wanted to ask him to come to dinner before the term was over and he left town. Mama agreed, so the date was set.

The dinner was a regular home-cooked meal served with mountain hospitality. There was a hen baked with dressing, creamed Irish potatoes, hot biscuits, home-canned pickled peaches, and salad consisting of lettuce, onions, and radishes from the garden. The dessert was homemade ice cream and cake. Mama did not have a matching set of china, silver, or crystal, but she took her one "company" tablecloth and the few good pieces of tableware she did have and matched things up the best she could. Finding herself one napkin short, she got one of Papa's big white handkerchiefs, folded it neatly, and put it beside Bob's plate. "He'll never know the difference," she thought.

But she was mistaken, for when they were about half through the meal, Bob held up the article and said in a loud voice, "Say, is this a napkin or a handkerchief?" Otherwise, Mama felt that the children were well-behaved for the company dinner, and she noticed that both Mary and Joe seemed to be enjoying themselves.

At Tarpley College in 1909 seniors did not wear caps and gowns for graduation. The boys wore dark suits and the girls white dresses, made just alike. That year the class has chosen organdy for the dress material. The pattern called for a high neckline, very full sleeves, and gathered skirts. The collars and cuffs were edged with lace and there were insets of it in the bodices. The girls were thrilled with their dresses and eagerly looked forward to preening themselves across the stage on graduation day. Then they learned with a shock that Marcella Jones's father had forbidden her to wear her organdy dress because one could see the flesh on her arms and neck through the sheer material. Such immodesty was unthinkable to him and he refused to listen to his daughter's pleas. When Marcella's classmates heard about the difficulty, they were up in arms, determined that she not be left out. They got together and created a pattern to make a bodice out of broadcloth. It had long, tight-fitting sleeves and a high neck. With the addition underneath the organdy, there was no "see-through," and Mr. Jones, deciding his daughter's modesty was preserved, allowed her to go on with the others.

Mama and Papa, proud of their eldest daughter's achievement, brought the family to the graduation. Mary was elated to be graduating, of course, but the fact that she had been fortunate enough to find a place to teach in an elementary school just seven miles from Tarpley was much more of a thrill to her.

A summer with no specially planned vacation trips might seem unendurable to another generation, but to the Barker family it differed not at all. They looked forward to summer, to the overnight visits of friends and cousins, to spending several days at a time with aunts and uncles, to picnics and ice cream suppers at the church, and finally to the family reunion which took place the first Sunday in August each year. This get-together assembled family members who had moved to different localities. From North Carolina they had emigrated to most of the states in the South and West. This year Oklahoma, Oregon, Georgia, and Texas were represented and the clan spirit was evident. Mama enjoyed the reunion along with everyone else, but she thought she could do without some of the extra company the occasion brought.

5

Coming home from school one sunny autumn day soon after the term had started, Jane was happy as a lark. Her friend Jud had asked her to join a group for a picnic on top of Hamburg Mountain. They were to make sandwiches, hike up the mountain, build a bonfire, and watch the sunset. Jane was so excited at the prospect that she rushed to tell Mama.

She found Mama lying on the bed with a towel folded across her forehead. Apparently she was "undone," as she called it, with a migraine headache. Jane knew quite well there would be no picnic, and although she was sorry for Mama, she resented having to change her plans. She went to her room, changed clothes, and stalked into the disordered kitchen where she stoically proceeded to put things to rights and begin preparations for the evening meal.

Some weeks later Mama was alone in the house when Jane came home from school. After greeting her, Mama said diffidently, "I guess you have noticed that we're going to have an addition to the family."

"Well, yes I have," admitted Jane, "and I'm awfully sorry."

"Why," countered Mama, "don't you believe it's the Lord's will for us to have another baby?"

"I think the Lord had some help with this one," said Jane sarcastically.

"That is irreverent," said Mama reprovingly, "and I'm surprised at you."

"It may be" said Jane, "but I can't help it. You have had enough children and you're too old. People won't know whether you are parents or grandparents when they see you with a baby. And another thing, I just wish Papa had to have this baby!"

Jane knew she had not been very kind to Mama and she was ashamed for having given way to her feelings. She knew she was lucky to have the kind of parents she had, too. They weren't too demanding or overstrict, and they didn't resort to physical punishment as some parents she knew were wont to do. She resolved to be more respectful in the future. "But darn it all," she said to herself. "It just isn't fair. Mama gets the worst of everything. She must have the baby and then she has to be up with it at night so she doesn't get enough rest to do all the things she has to do. One thing is for sure—I never intend to have eight children!"

On a snowy night in mid-February Jane was wakened by unusual noises, which of course she understood. She knew she was not to leave her room unless she was called for, so she sank back into a semiconscious state. The next morning family members were informed that they had a new baby brother named Daniel.

He was like a new toy to the younger children. As soon as they arrived from school they made a beeline for his crib and expressed disappointment if he was sleeping. Jane at first was aloof and stand-offish, but one afternoon she went to see him and found him lying in his crib trying to catch his own hands and cooing to himself. Involuntarily she exclaimed, "Oh, you little cutie!" Then she admitted to herself, "And to think, I didn't even want him!"

The rest of the winter was a hard one. With six children in school and a baby to care for, Mama had no leisure. But with all that, she was worried about Papa. She knew he was finding it increasingly difficult to provide for the needs of his growing family. Farmers still patronized the blacksmith shop, but in the last five years automobiles had penetrated even the mountain fastnesses of the Blue Ridge and

more and more people were discarding their horses and converting their stables into "car barns." Papa was pessimistic. "The automobile will ruin this country, just you wait and see," he predicted.

Meanwhile, Jane was in a world of her own. At sixteen she was receiving for the first time in her life marked attention from a young man. Jud walked with her back and forth from school, sat with her in church on Sunday, and escorted her to all available school functions. She fell deeply and wholeheartedly in love.

One afternoon she took Danny out for an airing in his carriage. On the way down the street, she met Jud and they walked along together. A tourist couple out for a stroll stopped them and the woman exclaimed, "What a beautiful baby. But you to look awfully young to be parents." Jane assured her that the baby was her brother, and as they walked on she laughed at the incident. To her surprise, however, Jud was not amused.

One weekend Jud made no effort to get in touch with her. Jane was at first irritated and then worried. She thought of calling his dorm, but she knew Mama would disapprove of such forward behavior. On Monday she went to school certain that Jud would explain his sudden behavior. Instead she saw a classmate who said, "Guess what? When my brother went to Asheville on Saturday, he saw Jud with Jessie Baldwin. They seemed to be having a high old time."

Jane fled to the sanctuary of the library where she could let the news sink in. She had trusted him so completely and believed that they would always love each other. She was sure her heart was broken and she would never be happy again.

For days she went around mechanically doing her duties, often giving way to tears after her younger sisters had gone to sleep. Mama understood what was happening and finally had a talk with Jane. She told her that often a young girl was in love with love, not a person, especially not a person who had a roving eye and whose fancy often changed. Such a person was usually in love with himself, unsettled, and immature. Mama assured Jane that she was too young to get serious with a man and that she should think of her disappointment as a learning experience.

Jane didn't think Mama knew much about such things, although she thought it good of her to be so sympathetic. Eventually Jud came back to see her and tried to patch things up, but Jane knew the magic was gone.

6

Nate, two years older than Jane, was behind her in school. He was a pitcher on the baseball team and one of Tarpley's best tennis players. It seemed that he was much more interested in sports than in his studies. When Jane or Mama tried to encourage him to pay more attention to his required classes, he usually said, "What's the big hurry? There's plenty of time."

Then one Saturday afternoon, like a bolt from the blue, tragedy struck the Barker family.

From time to time Nate did any odd jobs available to make what he called his "spending money." A distant cousin operated a farm just outside Tarpley and he needed some help harvesting a crop of corn for ensilage. Nate was given the job of feeding the stalks into a shredder which then went into a silo. While he was working, the cuff of his leather glove was caught by a stalk, pulling his hand into the shredder. In a matter of seconds, his arm was torn and mangled to the elbow.

Papa, white-faced and weak, came into the house to tell the rest of the family about the tragedy. He had been summoned immediately to the scene of the accident, and when he had seen Nate's blood-spattered clothes and mangled arm, he had cried out, "My God, Nate. Oh my God!" and had turned aside to be sick. He himself had ridden with his son in the ambulance to the hospital in Asheville. The doctor had told him that an emergency operation was necessary, and Papa had given his permission for Nate's right arm to be amputated just above the elbow.

The family listened to the news of the horrible accident as though they were in a daze. Finally Mama said, "We must all be brave and thank the Lord his life was saved."

"But Mama," exclaimed Mary. "What can he do with just one arm? What will become of him?" All the Barkers mourned for the one whose interest in sports had been the ruling obsession of his life. It was almost as if he had died.

A few nights later as the family sat around the supper table, Mama knew she must discuss the crisis facing them the next day when Nate was scheduled to come home from the hospital. "When he gets here," said Mama, "nobody must notice his bandaged arm. We must smile and welcome him as if he had been on a vacation, and there must be no tears."

When there was a general protest that it would be impossible not to notice his empty sleeve, Mama was firm. "We can do it and we must. He is the one who will have to learn to live without his arm, and I think it would be selfish and weak of us if we can't muster enough courage to try to make his homecoming cordial and unemotional."

Four-year-old Danny climbed out of his chair and came to stand by Mama. He looked up into her face searchingly and said, "But Mama, when Nate comes home and is well again, his arm will grow back, won't it?"

Mama, her eyes swimming with tears, could not answer. She got up hastily and began to carry the dishes to the kitchen. Papa, his own eyes suspiciously moist, took Danny on his lap and held him.

On the following afternoon when Nate arrived looking surprisingly natural, glad to see everybody and happy to be home, no mention was made of his arm. According to Mama's instructions, everyone tried to think of some interesting bit of news to tell him. At supper Papa added to his usual blessing, "We thank you, Lord, that the family is united again," and the first hurdle was over.

As the days passed Nate proved to have a wonderful attitude about his fate. If he was in pain and frustrated because he could not accomplish something, he was not embittered and tried hard to be cheerful for Papa and Mama's sake. Knowing that he could no longer hope for a sports career, he decided he must concentrate his efforts on getting a diploma. "The way it looks now," he said, "the best thing for me to do is to get through school and become an 'old maid school teacher' like the rest of the Barkers."

Jane's graduation came and went almost unnoticed, and it was late June before she found a place to teach. Her situation was like Mary's—she would have the first three grades in a two-teacher school close to Tarpley, making the munificent sum of forty dollars a month. Nate and Janice were both scheduled to complete requirements for graduation the following year.

Nate was not unhappy during his last year in school. He had learned to dress himself and could even shave with a straight-edged razor and tie his own shoes. Mary had given him a special knife-and-

fork combination, which allowed him to feed himself. Then he discovered he could still play tennis, grasping the ball between his thumb and second and third fingers, tossing it in the air, and then in a second swing sending it smashing across the court with his racquet. He also resumed his baseball practice, using the stump of his arm for an anchor as he wound up to pitch the ball.

When another graduation ceremony rolled around, two Barkers were on the list. Janice, so gifted in music, was also honored by being named valedictorian. And the senior awarded the medal for making the most progress in public speaking was Nate Barker.

7

The Barkers, especially Mama, had looked forward to seeing half of their brood out of college. They visualized a period of time when financial burdens would lighten and they would have a breathing spell before the next quartet had to have tuition for their higher education. With four of them working, it ought to be easier!

But although no one needed tuition for the 1916-17 school year, the Barkers had a new set of worries. Tarpley was to have a light and power system installed, and Papa and Mama thought this was an opportunity they could not afford to miss. They also knew that finding money to pay for this improvement and others would not be easy. Mama knew that the children who were working would help with these extras, but she wished it could be done without asking them to contribute.

The first thing they added that summer was a bathroom on one end of the back porch. A window was cut on one side and a door led out to the porch. The fixtures were installed and an oil burning stove was connected with a tank for heating water. The bathroom, even for the six people now at home, was a luxury, especially during the summer. When winter came though, with an occasional "cold snap," it was not unusual for the Barkers to revert to the zinc tub behind the kitchen range.

Shortly thereafter, the electric lights were installed. The house, built as it was, made it necessary for the wiring to run inside the rooms, all exposed to view. It was not an aesthetic improvement, but even so, nobody wanted to go back to using the smelly oil lamps or to take up the task of washing smoked lamp chimneys, with the daily chores of trimming wicks and filling the lamps with oil.

Late one afternoon Mama sat alone on the porch, ignoring the sunset which on other occasions she would have called magnificent. She was not relaxing either. She was confused, realizing to her dismay that she had been so determined in her single-minded way to accomplish a certain goal that she had lost sight of other things. First there was Papa, whose blacksmith shop clearly would soon be a thing of the past. Already he was opening it only on weekends, spending the rest of his time working as a carpenter in a construction company. Mama still felt guilty about insisting that he move away from

Swannanoa, and this decline in business surely did not make him any happier about being in Tarpley.

Then there was Mary. She had decided she no longer wanted to teach. She had been offered a scholarship to Columbia University in New York City and was sure she would die if she didn't get to go. When she got a degree in home economics, then she would be eligible to become a home demonstration agent—that was the big thing in North Carolina now, with every county having an agent—and she would be much better paid than if she taught.

Papa had said, "But, Mary, the scholarship won't pay all your expenses. You'll have to borrow money. Why don't you stay here and teach a few years, then get married and have a family of your own?"

"Papa, with all the brothers and sisters I've had around me all my life, I don't want to start another family," Mary had replied, apparently determined to continue her education.

Then there was Bob. Reluctantly Mama admitted that in all likelihood slow moving, good natured Bob was not likely to graduate from any high school, much less college. Papa would just have to help him get some kind of job, maybe as a carpenter. She knew it was not logical, but she felt it was impossible to have borne a child who didn't share her ambition and desire to finish school. It just didn't bear thinking about.

Mama was realizing that all children were not alike just because they happened to be brothers and sisters. She was also becoming aware of the fact that her children were becoming young men and women with ideas and ambitions of their own, and not all of these coincided with hers.

It was time to cook supper, so she rose and went inside. She worked automatically at her chores, but her mind was still busy with her problems. She wanted to find something to help eke out their income. More and more women were working outside their home, and if the war that was being talked and written about materialized, still more women would be needed. Trying to think of places that might be open to women, she recalled that practically all milliners were women—but she couldn't trim hats! She could not work in a laundry or a bakery or a restaurant because she couldn't stay away from home such long hours. Maybe she could write a book, but, also, maybe she couldn't. The only things she could write about would be those she had actually experienced—prosaic, ordinary happenings which nobody would read about. She had no imagination.

It had been in the back of her mind all along, but now she was ready to acknowledge that she meant to try to teach school again. She didn't think Papa would approve, so she decided she would turn things over in her mind awhile before she told him about her plans. Papa could be very abrupt at times. She remembered an evening they had spent with friends and the subject of women's suffrage had come up. She expressed herself as being in favor of it and said she looked forward to the time when women could vote. Papa had said very positively, "Now Cora, you are old enough to know that women's place is in the home." Mama thought a woman's place was in the home as long as the children needed her, but after they all went to school, she decided that a woman's place was wherever she could find a place.

8

Jane's year of teaching a few miles from Tarpley convinced her that she truly enjoyed her work but she didn't like living at home now that she was able to support herself. She wanted to get away for awhile and be on her own, so she was very pleased to be offered a job in the extreme northeastern section of North Carolina. It was five hundred miles from Tarpley and within ten miles of the Atlantic Ocean.

As excited as Jane was to get this school, she was unprepared for all the changes she encountered. Born and reared in the Carolina mountains, she knew no landscape but hills that curved up and down with unexpected level valleys bordering clear streams, and, in the distance, fresh green hills with the soft blue mountains forming a background beyond them. Boarding the train in the afternoon, she watched the shifting scenery until nightfall. When she awoke the next morning in her Pullman berth, she looked out the window and was amazed that the land stretched away as far as the eye could see, flat as the palm of her hand.

A trustee of the school met Jane at the depot and drove her the seven miles to Cranston, the little community where she would be teaching. The sandy road, stretching straight as an arrow, was bordered on both sides by great fields of cotton and peanuts. Jane, accustomed to red clay hills, thought this soil looked unproductive, but she had to admit eventually that the crops she saw were growing lustily. The trustee told her that many of the peanut fields had single furrows over a mile long without a single curve in them.

Jane received a warm welcome from the Cranston community. Many of the patrons called on her and often she was invited to Sunday dinner by the parents of some of her pupils. On Saturday nights there was usually a gathering of the young working people in somebody's house. Jane had worried that she might be homesick, but she was far too busy with her schoolwork and socializing even to think about home much.

She threw herself into her work, gradually becoming accustomed to the strange landscape and peculiar accents. People in the eastern part of the state talked so differently that she kept a notebook of localisms she had never heard before, such as, "He chunked a rock right through the window," and, "That was some kind of pretty," and, "I thought you won't going to town today." Once when she was telling her class that she had never seen big fields of peanuts or the blooms and balls of a cotton stalk before, a serious looking little boy raised his hand. "If you don't have any peanuts and cotton, how do people make a living?" he asked.

Jane tried to explain that cattle raising and truck farming, such as apples, hay, and corn, were the principal ways of making a living in her part of the state, but he still looked puzzled. "I guess he won't understand until he sees it himself," she thought.

One of the young people Jane met at the first Saturday night party was Boyd Brock. She had been flattered by the attention he had paid her ever since, but after her experience with Jud she had treated him very cautiously. Her reluctance to accept his invitations seemed to make him all the more eager to be with her, and he was a frequent visitor at the teacherage.

On a lovely spring afternoon Boyd asked Jane to ride with him down to the beach. He was driving a shiny rubber-tired buggy and they skimmed along the smooth sandy roads with ease. Sometimes there were palm trees bordering the way; sometimes at the edge of

a swampy place the tall cypress trees stood with their knees sticking up out of the brackish water.

When they reached the little town, Boyd left his horse and buggy at the livery stable and the couple set out on foot to explore the premises. They walked along the beach, gathered some sea oats, and came back by a drug store where they got sandwiches and milkshakes. Suddenly Jane realized it was getting late and she must be back at her boarding house before twilight. She didn't dare be out driving with a young man after dark.

During the return trip Boyd said to her, without any preamble or warning, "You know, I've been thinking, and I believe it would be a good thing for you and I to get married."

Jane didn't take him seriously. "For you and I?" she asked him archly. "Don't you mean 'for you and me'?"

"I mean for you and I," he answered positively. "I like the sound of it that way. And I mean what I'm saying and I want you to think about it, too. If you do, I believe I can convince you that I am right."

"Well, what am I to do—say 'This is so sudden' and fall into a swoon?"

"You faint? Well, I'm from Missouri! But if you do, I'll catch you, and when you 'come to' just remember what I have said."

The conversation was not pursued during the rest of the ride back to Cranston, but the subject came up again the following Sunday. Jane and Boyd went to church together, and because it was a second Sunday there was dinner on the grounds and almost everyone in the Cranston area went to church.

A good number of automobiles were parked out front, but the patch of woods at the back of the church still held buggies and horses, the mode of transportation for a large percentage of the congregation. Boyd had taken his horse from the buggy and tied him in a shady spot. The buggy he left at the edge of the woods, as he said, for propriety's sake so that everyone could see what was going on.

The trestle tables were loaded with delicacies on which a multitude could have fed. After going up and down the tables, leisurely taking samples from dishes and making conversation with the folks who had prepared them, Boyd said to Jane. "If I keep this up I'll be kissing all the babies and hugging all the grandmas just like a real politician."

"Don't tell me you were bored," said Jane. "You loved it all! I had to stand aside and be the staid school marm while you were the Prince Charming!"

"That's just what I've been trying to tell you," he answered. "That's one of the reasons why we ought to get married. I know I get carried away sometimes and am irresponsible, but you are sedate and practical and matter of fact. You need me to loosen you up a bit and I need you to nail me down when I get out of hand!"

As he left her late that afternoon he said, "I've enjoyed this day. We must go to church somewhere real soon where they'll have dinner on the grounds again."

But it didn't happen that way.

The next week Boyd called unannounced to see Jane. They sat in Mrs. Tilson's parlor with its organ, horsehair sofa, and starched lace curtains. He had come to tell her that he was being called into the army and in a few days must report to Camp Sevier in Greenville, South Carolina.

Jane was stunned. She knew the war was going on, but it was far away and had not touched her family yet. Papa was too old, Nate was ineligible, and Bob was too young. A lot of her friends and associates were in the service and a great many were already in France. Of course, everyone out of uniform was questioned. She remembered that at a party one night, when Boyd was asked why he hadn't gone, he had replied impudently that he was a conscientious objector. Another time when the subject was broached, he had said he was a Four F because of a brain defect. Boyd had made it all appear like a big joke then, but tonight he was different. He told her, "If I said I wanted to go I'd be lying. I don't like anything about the army and I dread going. I can't help wondering why America feels she must be mixed up in all those European nations who are trying to kill each other. But I am no better than all the fellows who have had to go before me. So, now that my turn has come, I'll do my best."

Jane didn't want to be serious. She was afraid she might cry, and she did not share the generally accepted idea that tears were a woman's prerogative and her best weapon. For her, they were a sign of weakness, and she had often told herself when she was disturbed, "I'm too big to cry." So, she said to Boyd instead, "Oh, I know you! You won't be in France long before you will have found yourself a pretty little mademoiselle and you'll forget all about me!"

"Sure, I'll be on the lookout for a little Frenchie," Boyd replied. "But don't you worry—when it's over I'll be back and a certain little hillbilly had better be waiting for me!"

9

Back in Tarpley, things were on the mend. Mama made peace with Papa about trying to go back to teaching. She had reviewed the textbooks she needed for the teacher's examination, and shortly after she took it, she received word that she had earned a creditable rating. Her first applications for a place to teach were disappointing since no one seemed to have an opening, especially for someone as old as she was. But she kept trying, and, finally, she heard of a one-teacher school "around the mountain" from Tarpley, at Allman's Cove, where the teacher had resigned because of illness. Mama lost no time getting to the trustees to offer her services, and, since they did not want the school term interrupted, they asked if she could begin on Monday. Although that schedule gave Mama only the weekend to get ready, she consented. She hurried home with the news and after supper had a family conference. The chores were divided so that each person was allowed, as much as possible, to choose the things he or she liked best to do.

Bob could not be counted on for as much as the girls, for he was doing odd jobs for people when he could. Just now, he was working with Papa as a carpenter's helper, but he was assigned the tasks of keeping the kitchen woodbox filled and of looking after the Warm Morning heater which had replaced the fireplace in the dining room. In the winter time the whole family used that room as a sitting room.

Millie, always dependable and good-natured, was to be responsible for Danny from the time his school was out until Mama could get home in the afternoon. She would share the bedmaking, dishwashing, and ironing with Susan. Susan would also see that the pantry had the essential staples for cooking, but Mama would still be the cook, taking over the kitchen at night.

While these plans were being made, Papa sat in his easy chair, engaged with the newspaper. He was content for Mama and the children to work out these plans on paper, where they sounded easy. If she was determined to go back to teaching, Papa thought, let her work it out.

On Monday morning Mama cooked her usual breakfast of sausage, eggs, hot biscuits, butter, and jelly. When she had her brood

at the table, she fixed a lunch pail for Papa and Bob, made herself a sandwich for lunch, hastily threw on her clothes, and made off for school. Bob had hitched up old Dixie to the now creaking buggy. Mama piled in with her books, a bundle of kindling, a kettle, a sack of oats for Dixie, and some odds and ends of school materials her older children had used and discarded. In spite of all the trouble in getting off to school, Mama was in a cheerful mood. With her experience with children of all ages, she felt confident that she could handle this group. Also, she admitted to herself that she was looking forward to being out of the house several hours a day, even if she might have to work longer hours to keep things going.

Mama had never studied psychology, but she had a good understanding of human nature. It did not take her long to spot the school bully, the smart aleck, and the troublemakers among her students. She saw to it that the bully left the small children alone, and she could squelch the smart aleck with a look, but as she did so she tried to make friends with all the students. She told them that every pupil must cooperate if they were to have a successful school, and that she needed their help.

Of course, these generally considered roughnecks in Allman's Cove did not turn into perfect students overnight. Mama had her problems. She was not always able to forestall unpleasant situations that sometimes marred a day, but as time went on, things improved. The pupils responded to her sincere efforts and she soon had allies willing to work with her.

The twenty-five students of assorted ages and scattered in grades from one to seven all in one room presented a challenge to Mama. She planned her schedule so she could have two, three, and sometimes four classes going at the same time. She tried to do most of her teaching to the ones in the sixth and seventh grades and to the five and six-year-olds who were beginners. Under her direction and with her lesson plans, some of the larger pupils could take charge of certain classes.

She had a box of soil placed in one corner of the room and in it the students experimented with seedlings and rooted cuttings. On Friday afternoon they had varied activities—one Friday a spelling bee, the next a hike to a nearby waterfall and a picnic supper, another a program of original compositions. These were written by the older children describing some lesson they had liked (or disliked). Mama picked out poems that she thought all children should know and had the pupils memorize and recite them by turns. On the last Friday before Thanksgiving, she took from home a big frying pan and the ingredients for making dough. Some of her pupils brought dried apples already cooked and seasoned. She kept four students inside to help her cook (two boys and two girls, since Mama firmly believed that boys should know how to cook) and excused the others to go hunting or identifying autumn leaves on the school grounds. Mama and her four helpers made and fried dried apple turnovers on the big iron stove. They were hot and delicious and made a great feast for the children.

The stove had a broken leg and was propped up on bricks, and there were other things wrong with the schoolroom. A few window-panes were missing. New blackboards and chalk were needed. There was no money allotted for school supplies and Mama decided she would have to do something about it.

She discussed the matter with the trustees and they encouraged her to have a box supper. Notes were sent to all the parents urging them to come and to invite others in the community. The school room was decorated with holly, fir, and spruce boughs and looked very attractive. A trustee was the auctioneer and the boxes were promptly sold. After supper, word games were played in which all could take part. The evening ended with a string band from the cove playing old familiar songs for a community sing.

Mama was elated with the results. There was money enough to take care of the most pressing needs, and she had a warm feeling of gratitude for the patrons who had helped to make the evening a success. Even Papa and Danny had gone along with her. She knew Papa would never openly admit it, but she was sure he had had a good time! Danny thought it was great and said so repeatedly. After hearing the string band play, he decided he needed a banjo, too.

Having a job made a world of difference to Mama. She had been tired of the house with its unrelenting chores, and although she had been on a merry-go-round since she had started school, she enjoyed the change and felt she was more a part of what was going on around her. In the past, she had also grown oh so weary of having to ask for every cent she received. Now, small as her salary was, it helped and Mama was able to give money to her own children for incidentals. She was ever so happy with her teaching.

10

Christmas of 1917 was to be a quiet affair. For the first time in twenty-six years, all the members of the family would not be home for the holidays. Mary, in New York, was doing some clerical work in addition to her classes, and would only have a few days off from work. Jane, in Cranston, had decided the trip would be too expensive for her to make. Still, that left eight people to look out for, so Mama didn't really expect a vacation.

Christmas would be quiet for other reasons. The war had taken thousands of young men overseas and already there were some who would not come back. Mama said she felt sad every time she saw a young man in uniform. The preacher said, "There shall be wars and rumors of wars," but she didn't believe they should go on forever, especially when to her it seemed the fighting came about because one country decided it should have some land that belonged to another settled nation.

Christmas Day came. The Barker family had all hung up their stockings and they enjoyed opening presents before the usual Christmas feast. Then they sat around the fire, popped popcorn, and played games until bedtime. The surprise came the next day, when they awoke to look out on a white world and a howling blizzard. It had piled snow high in drifts and paralyzed traffic. To add to the discomfort, it was bitterly cold, and the family was housebound. "Storms like this belong to New England, not as far south as the Carolinas," Mama thought.

The first day or two went splendidly. They made a huge snowman and had a few snowball fights. Once a day they wrapped up warmly and walked to the post office. The young folks were invited to a friend's home to a "candy pulling." Homemade molasses was boiled on top of the stove until it thickened. After it was cooled enough to be handled, a mass of it was given to each couple who faced each other and pulled together. After a while the candy stiffened, and then it was broken in short lengths and called "stick candy."

One night after supper they all sat around the fire while Papa read aloud "Snowbound" by John Greenleaf Whittier. They all thought it was a very appropriate poem for such an occasion. By the end of the week the poem seemed too much like their own situation. Everyone began to seem edgy and get on each other's nerves. They felt restless and housebound and even looked forward to the end of vacation.

When the new year was ushered in and the weather improved, they were soon back on the same old merry-go-round. Papa was working in Asheville, which was fast becoming a tourist attraction. One hotel after another was under construction. For transportation he had to commute on the little interurban streetcar line which ran from Tarpley to Asheville, and he carried his lunch with him. Bob had gone to Knoxville, where he was staying with Papa's brother Jim. He was taking a six-month training course to work as a garage mechanic. Only the three younger children were at home. It made Mama feel lonely to think of how quickly her brood had scattered. Although she kept as busy as ever, she missed each one of her absent children daily.

The cold winter of 1917 ended in time, and the spring of 1918 was lovely, but people were more and more conscious of the war going on. Jane wrote that Boyd was still in camp and feeling resentful because he had not been sent overseas. In the midst of war, one can hardly realize just what is happening, and since news of a battle came by cable or appeared a day or two late in the newspaper, no one could predict the duration of the outcome of this supposed "war to end wars." Mama thought Jane was more interested in Boyd than she would admit even to herself, and it made her anxious. She wondered what he really was like and if he would be another "ladies' man" with a roving fancy like Jud. She wished she could see Jane and talk to her.

When school ended in May, Mama went into an orgy of house cleaning. She washed windows, laundered curtains, sunned quilts and mattresses, mopped floors and scrubbed the wide planks of the kitchen floor until they were spotless, hung the carpet from the parlor on the clothesline, and beat the dust out of it with a broom. Mama was proud of this carpet, even though Susan often complained that it did not have flowers like those other people had. Grandma Patton had made the parlor carpet out of old clothing cut in strips and sewn together. Then she had woven the strips on a big loom which stood in the corner of her kitchen. It took fifteen square yards of carpeting for the parlor, and Mama had forgotten how long it had taken Grandma to make it.

Soon Janice and Jane arrived for their summer vacations, but Nate was not to be with them. He had a job offer as a desk clerk in a hotel in the town where he had been teaching and was quite happy with it. Although everyone missed Nate, it was a lively household without him. They made up teams for the daily chores: Mama and Danny took the kitchen garden and what they called the front yard, Millie and Susan chose the house cleaning, and Janice and Jane did the cooking. They all shared the washing and ironing.

The Barkers had recently acquired a washing machine, a forerunner of electric machines but infinitely easier to operate than the scrubbing board. The hand-operated machine stood on four legs, supporting a tub with a rounded bottom in which a wooden inset called a cradle rocked back and forth over the soapy clothes. Attached to one side of the washer was a hand-turned wringer, which saved a lot of hard wrist work but was also a grand place to catch the buttons of a garment at the wrong angle and snap them off. Danny called it the button buster.

Practically all the young men the age of Jane and Janice were away in service, but the girls did not seem to mind. Jane spent a good part of her vacation in summer school, earning extra credits necessary for a pay raise. Janice belonged to a string band which played for various social activities and often gave open air concerts in the park on Sunday afternoons. Susan saw to it that the Barker house had some teenagers in evidence. Millie, the agreeable one, often went along on Susan's outings. She told Janice she was Susan's chaperone.

Danny was the one Mama was concerned about. One would think that the youngest child in a big family would be very lucky. He'd have older brothers and sisters to spoil him, give up to him, and provide things they did not have at his age. But it did not always work out that way. Being so much younger than the others, he was like an only child who had to grow up alone and, as Danny said, had more bosses than any one person could ever get along with. So she and Danny worked together in the vegetable garden and in cleaning up the premises, and she encouraged him to have boys his age over for an afternoon.

Millie and Susan were constantly singing the war songs—"Over There," "It's a Long Way to Tipperary," "K-K-K-Katie," and "Keep the Home Fires Burning." They had also learned a new game called "Rook," and on summer evenings they often had a table or two going. Some preferred dominoes, some checkers, but everybody liked Rook. Papa was shocked when someone told him that Rook was played just like regular cards. Simple substitutions had been made— fourteen for an ace, thirteen for a king, twelve for a queen, and eleven for a jack. He was undecided as to whether he should allow this game in his house. He remembered very well that he had promised his father to have nothing to do with playing cards, and to him it was unthinkable to break that promise. The children, however, were able to convince him that the numbers had no relations to the wicked emblems, and the game went on.

Mama thought she must have been born lucky, or at least she sometimes did have a lucky break, like the one that came late that summer. A lot of teachers were leaving the classrooms since the war had opened new and better paying jobs for women. When one of the teachers in Tarpley Elementary left to work for the Red Cross, the trustees offered the place to Mama.

Her new position solved many problems. She felt that she had proved she could teach and still carry on at home. She would be teaching in the same school that Danny attended, and even though he was not in her grade, she could keep an eye on him. Susan was entering Tarpley College in September, and Millie was to be a junior. The outlook seemed bright for a pleasant and peaceful school year.

When Papa had sold the farm in Swannanoa and had bought the house in Tarpley, there had been a little money left over. With it he had invested in forty acres of land about one mile outside Tarpley. It was poor, unproductive, and neglected, but it was cheap. They had named it the Briar Patch, and it was a special favorite for all the family for many kinds of outings. Some apple trees still produced a crop in the fall, and there were chestnut trees and chinquapin bushes and wild grapevines—all of which attracted the children and young people.

One Sunday afternoon in September, Mama and Papa took a basket and decided to walk over to the Briar Patch to get some wild grapes for making jelly. It was a warm September afternoon. The goldenrod and Joe Pye weed vied with the red of the dogwood leaves and sourwood. The clear yellow of the hickory trees added their contrast. They walked to the little spring which flowed from under the mountain and sat down on a big flat stone beside the small stream that trickled from the spring. The grapes were on the mountain side, and they needed to get their breath before they started the climb. Also, they were thirsty.

"There's no water anywhere else that tastes like cold spring water," Papa said after his second drink as he wiped his forehead with his handkerchief and hung the gourd dipper back in its place on the spring house wall. They climbed the steep hill to the woods where the grapevines were. The crop was bountiful and hung heavy and ripe so that their basket was soon filled.

"Oh, drat it all," said Mama when she surveyed the tear in her stockings which the brambles had snagged as she walked by. "I wish I had worn pants."

Papa looked at her with mischief in his eyes and answered, "You wear the pants in this family anyhow, Cora."

"If I do, I surely wish I'd had them on today. It would have saved my stockings."

The Briar Patch was situated in a little valley, and they had another climb to make to get back to the highway. When they got to the top of the knoll they stood to take in the view. At the horizon were outlined three blue mountains almost exactly the same size and shape, and at that distance they seemed identical. They were known as the Three Sisters. The dark green of the pine forest was interposed between the blue range and the trees tinged with early fall colors. The sun was setting with the rosy orange of an autumn sunset. It was a glorious view and an enchanted moment in their lives. Not given much to talking, they stood there drinking in the beauty of their surroundings and sharing with each other a sense of peace and well-being.

11

In November the armistice was signed and even small towns like Tarpley celebrated exuberantly. Bells rang, whistles blew, bands played, schools were dismissed, and the children marched in parades up the streets. The world, as all were told, was about to begin an existence where brotherhood was foremost and there would be no more war.

Schoolwork seemed easier than it had been the year before, and the weeks slipped by. Mama said she had better keep her fingers crossed, for just as surely as she thought that everything was moving smoothly for them, some sort of calamity befell the family or some unexpected problem arose.

Soon the predicted calamity showed itself. A letter from Bob told them he was about through with his training course, and he was sure he would get a job. Also, he had met a girl he liked a lot and they decided that they wanted to get married—he knew Papa and Mama would understand that he needed some money.

"Heavens above!" exclaimed Papa. "He's only nineteen years old and evidently doesn't even have a job. What in the world can he be thinking of?"

Mama mourned to herself, "He's planned to be exactly what I was trying so hard to spare my children from becoming—a day laborer with little hope of advancement."

They decided to write Bob immediately, asking him to come home for a visit and let them talk things over before he took such a step. The next morning the letter was dispatched, and they waited with some apprehension for an answer.

About a week later the answer came. Bob thought it would be a good idea to come home, and he was planning to do so. He and Lula had thought it would be easier all around if they got married and came together so that is what they had done. He had bargained for an old secondhand car and was trying to "patch it up" so they could travel in it. He would let them know when to expect them.

Neither Papa nor Mama was the sort of person to go into a tirade or have hysterics when receiving such a shock. They read the letter and sat in stunned silence trying to realize just what was happening.

Mama noticed that at the bottom of the page Bob had written "(over)." She turned the letter over and on the back he had added, "Lula's Mama is coming with us."

That weekend Bob, Lula, and Mrs. Drake arrived. Millie gave up her room to Bob and Lula and moved in with Susan, while Mrs. Drake occupied the only spare bedroom in the house. Mama comforted the girls by saying, "It will only be for a few days," but as she made the statement she knew deep inside that she was only trying to convince herself and hoping against hope that the situation was not as grim as it seemingly was going to be.

The affairs of the family continued without interruption. Everyone got up in the mornings, did the chores, and went their separate ways for the day's occupations. Bob, Lula, and Mrs. Drake stayed at the house, apparently quite satisfied. They made themselves very much at home. One week went by, then another, and still another. Mama and Papa were feeling the strain. They felt helpless and depressed. Bob had not only ignored their advice, but also he had brought to their house two complete strangers, who apparently intended to spend the winter. Of course, Bob didn't realize what he was doing, but Mama's philosophy was the same as always, "I don't know what in the world we can do, but I know we've simply got to do something!"

Papa took Bob out and talked to him. "Son, you said you were ready to go to work. Are you trying to find yourself a job?"

"I aim to pretty soon," Bob answered.

"I think you'd better start right today. You have taken on the responsibility of looking after somebody besides yourself and how are you going to do that without a job?"

"I thought we would stay with you a little while."

"That was all right for a while, but we can't take on three extra people to house and feed indefinitely. You must know that. Now, you find yourself something to do, and Mama and I will help you get enough things together to go to housekeeping. I suppose your mother-in-law will be going back home soon, won't she?"

"I-I don't know," Bob said weakly.

"Well, one thing at a time," Papa said. "You see if one of the garages will hire you and then we will make some further plans."

When Bob did find a job in a garage a couple of miles up the highway, Papa and Mama went to see a widow who lived nearby and had rooms to let. There were two large rooms with an outside entrance through a side porch. While it was not built for a kitchen, the owner was willing for them to use one of the rooms for that purpose and suggested that they buy a two-burner oil stove for cooking. When they took Bob and Lula to look at the rooms, there was little excitement or anticipation evident. Both seemed confused and bewildered as they looked around.

Lula said, "Two rooms is not enough for three people."

Mama said, "Well, maybe Mrs. Drake will rent another room for herself."

"But she can't afford to do that," Lula answered. "She only has enough for her clothes and doctor bills. She's not well, you know."

"In that case, I guess you'll have to start with two rooms anyway, since Bob can't afford to pay any more rent."

Papa and Mama got a wooden bedstead out of the attic, cleaned and polished it, and bought some coil springs and a mattress, since feather beds and straw ticks were no longer in vogue. They gave Bob the chest of drawers that had been in his room, found an old table or two, and bought the suggested oil stove for the kitchen. Bob had come up with a cot Mrs. Drake could use (and criticize), and the housekeeping experiment got under way. Mama's parting words to them were, "Remember, we want you to come have dinner with us on Sunday."

12

One December day in 1918, Jane was busy in her school room in Cranston. Her class was studying about the first settlements in America, and after she discovered that the story in the textbook had little meaning for the children, she decided to construct a sand table. They made log cabins out of cardboard and put deer, foxes, and rabbits in the forest. They were busy trying to decide the best place to put a church with a small steeple when there was a knock at the door. A pupil opened it and then turned to Jane to say, "There's someone to see you."

Jane pushed her hair back from her forehead and went to see who the caller was. A long arm pulled her unceremoniously out into the hall, closed the door, gave her a bear hug and a lusty kiss, and she leaned back to let her see where the whirlwind came from. It was Boyd. He opened the door and followed her into the room, and, while she was still trying to compose herself, she heard him say, "Aren't you going to introduce me?"

Without hesitating she announced, "Boys and girls, this is Mr. Brooks, who has just come home from France."

Then she added, hoping as she did to give him a bit of a shock in return, "Perhaps he would like to talk to you now."

For a second Boyd did seem startled, but he quickly recovered himself and with elaborate ceremony he felt in his coat pocket, in his pants pockets, and even in his vest pocket as if he were frantically searching for something. "You know," he said, "I had a speech all written out but I'm afraid I left it at home. So I'll just have to say hello to you boys and girls and tell you I hope that by the time you grow up there won't be any more wars and you'll never have to go fight in one."

As Boyd picked up his hat and started to leave the room, he passed by Jane and whispered, "I'll see you tonight."

That evening they sat in the swing on Mrs. Tilson's vine-covered porch. Boyd said, "I just can't believe it has happened—to realize that I could go where I have been, could slog through rain and mud in the trenches, hear the guns firing and all the other sounds of war—and then come through it all alive and land back here in Cranston.

But best of all was to find you in the schoolroom teaching the children just as if none of this had ever taken place. I didn't know how glad I was to be living until now!"

"Was it all so terrible? Weren't there some moments that were happier and less harrowing?"

"Well, of course," he said laughing. "There was the little French girl."

"Where is she now? What did you do with her?"

"Oh, I decided to leave her in France for the time being, and if I get bored with you I can go back for her later."

"Boyd Brooks, I wish I could hate you!" Jane said.

"But you don't and that's all that matters. I won't be coming back to Cranston to work now," Boyd continued. "The company is opening a new store in Charlotte, and I am going to be sent there. I have three weeks' vacation before I have to start, but there are a lot of things I have to get settled before I move. Number one—when can we get married? Number two—must I find an apartment or will you help me? Number three—when can we go see your parents?''

"Oh, Boyd, you make me dizzy—you move so fast. Why, you don't know much about me. Here you come back from the war driving a new car your Papa gave you, and if I were to get married my Papa couldn't even give me a wheelbarrow! I belong to a big family and we all have to work. A schoolteacher's salary doesn't allow many frills, I can tell you. So I'm not ready to get married—I couldn't buy three new dresses, let alone a trousseau!''

"That's all right, honey,'' Boyd said as he put his arm around her. "We don't need a wheelbarrow and the clothes you wear suit me just fine.''

Soon letters began coming to Tarpley from Cranston with increasing frequency. Bit by bit Mama and Papa learned that Boyd and Jane were planning to get married, that they wanted to come to Tarpley during Easter weekend, that Boyd was being transferred to a new store in Morgan Hill near Charlotte, that he would be manager, that they would stop over night in Durham with Mama's sister Mary, that they would leave Cranston on Friday morning and arrive in time for supper on Saturday night, and that they would be coming in the Ford roadster Boyd's parents had given him.

Mama wished they had had the house painted on the outside, where it needed it so badly. The inside also needed some refurbishing, but that was beyond them now. It didn't help matters to dwell on such things, and Mama had plenty to do trying to give the house a going-over and getting enough food ready to carry them through the weekend.

Good Friday came, and when the visitors had not arrived by dusk, the Barker family, already tired, grew cross. Millie said, "If they don't get here pretty soon, these rolls will be ruined. They've been ready to bake for nearly an hour.''

Mama was worried, too. She knew that there were few miles of paved roads outside city limits and that driving could be especially hazardous at night. But Danny brought up a complaint she hadn't thought about. "It's so dark now that nobody can see an automobile driving up to our house,'' he lamented.

The tension was relieved shortly, however, for Boyd and Jane arrived, the mud-splashed car and Boyd's muddy shoes and rumpled suit telling the story of their difficulties. Going over the highway between Old Fort and Asheville the travelers were twice bogged down in the mud so that they had to get a farmer with a team of mules to pull them out of the mire. When a shower came up, Boyd got out of the car to put up the curtains, and Jane, trying to be helpful, got out too so that she could hold an umbrella over his head while he worked. "The result was," said Boyd, "that by the time I got the curtains up it had stopped raining but Jane and I were both wet.

Millie's rolls were not ruined and the group was soon seated at the big table. Boyd's outgoing friendliness helped to put everybody at ease and the dinner was a good beginning for a pleasant weekend.

Boyd was a delightful guest. He played ball with Nate and Danny, he praised Millie's cooking, and he teased Susan about her boyfriends. To Mama and Papa he was very respectful and seemed quite sincere and straightforward when, late in the evening, he began his speech with "of course, you know why I am here" and explained that he wanted to marry Jane.

Papa and Mama, answering by turns, told Boyd they felt that Jane, being over twenty-one, was grown and was capable of making her own decision as to whom she would marry. They hoped she had made a wise choice, but if she were happy, that was all they asked.

Early Sunday morning Boyd and Jane started on their two-day journey back to Cranston. Jane would miss one day of school, but she had received permission to do that. Their anxiety centered on the condition of the roads over the mountain, but Boyd said, "We got through coming up, so we ought to make it going back."

Danny was pleased to note that it was light enough for the neighbors to see them drive away.

13

After school on Monday afternoon Mama came in and sat at the kitchen table enjoying a cup of coffee. She had a satisfied feeling about the weekend. It was one time, she thought, when everything clicked—it all seemed to go just right and the whole family had enjoyed the time spent together.

Susan interrupted her reverie. "I'm sure glad Bob and Lula had already gone back to Tennessee when Boyd came," she said.

"That isn't very loyal to your brother, is it?" asked Mama.

"Well, just what would we have done if Mrs. Drake has still been here in the guest room? Even after they got their apartment they always managed to get back here for the weekend—and you know it as well as I do. We need all the room we have. And don't forget that Janice told you she was coming home some weekend soon and wants to bring that band leader with the funny name. I think she is really stuck on him, don't you?"

"Oh, no, child," said Mama. "He's just a co-worker and a good friend. Besides, I'll bet he's old enough to be her father."

"I wouldn't count on his age having any effect on Janice if she likes him."

Mama got up to fix supper, and they dropped the conversation. She was too busy thinking about Jane and Boyd to worry about Janice. Although they planned to have a quiet and simple ceremony, they wanted it to be at home and that sort of wedding would keep the household busy.

Bit by bit the wedding plans progressed and the spring cleaning was accomplished. Mama declared she had two days of work to complete every single day. As a rule she looked forward to the end of her school day when she could relax and take things easy until time for the evening chores to begin. Now, by the time she hung up her hat, she had to start on the second stint of the day.

Boyd and Jane's wedding was set for early June and the scent of honeysuckle filled the air. Mama's roses were at their best and she had no need of a florist or hothouse flowers to decorate the rooms. One end of the big front porch was vine-covered, forming a sort of alcove where a double-seated swing hung. Removing the swing, they

48

arranged an altar there. Susan said that the guests would be seated on the veranda, too. "Yes," said Mama, "they will be seated on the front porch."

Jane, thought Mama, was a lovely bride—fresh looking, young, and natural. It didn't matter that she did not wear the traditional white satin wedding dress with a veil and train. She had wanted a practical sort of dress that she could wear after the ceremony and had chosen a pearl taffeta made with a pleated skirt and a draped bodice which ended with a wide sash tied in the back. The sleeves were of matching chiffon gathered full and caught at the wrist with bands of taffeta. With this she wore nine-inch grey kid boots that laced up in front and just touched the hem of her dress. Aunt Jessie had made it for her.

The guest list included Boyd's father and mother, the Barker family, a few aunts, uncles, and cousins, and the neighbors who lived on either side of the family. They couldn't be left out after they had lent chairs and dishes for the occasion. Immediately following the ceremony Susan and Millie served a buffet luncheon to the thirty-five who had filled the front porch.

When it was all over, Mama was tired but she didn't stop. There was furniture to be re-arranged, dishes to be returned, floors to be swept, and another meal to prepare. "I'm glad it's over with," she said to herself, "but it did go off well and seemed sort of sweet and sacred. How I do hope they will be happy!"

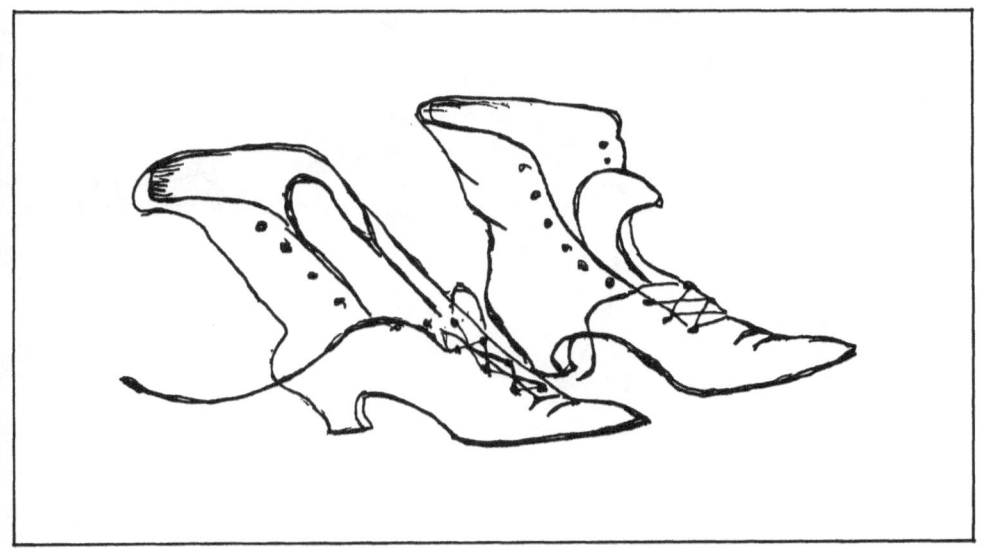

After Jane and Boyd left Mama had a sort of lonely feeling. It was the first time Jane wouldn't be spending her summer vacation at home. Since North Carolina schools had terms of only seven or eight months, the young teachers often had four or five months to stay at home. Mary, Nate, and Bob had jobs year round, but Jane and Janice had always spent the summer months in Tarpley, and both Mama and Papa had enjoyed having the children return. Mama comforted herself by saying, "At least Janice will be home and she will liven things up for all of us."

The following week Janice came but Mama's pleasure was short-lived. Janice was bubbling over with enthusiasm because she had learned that she had won a scholarship to attend a summer course for public school music teachers at the University in Knoxville. She had hardly unpacked her suitcases before she was busy repacking them to go away again. It also developed that Pete Lovorini was to be among the students in the summer session.

Mama admitted that she was uneasy. She had convinced herself that Janice's liking for this middle-aged band leader was the result of propinquity as well as the love they shared for music, but now it was different. When Lovorini had visited their home earlier in the year, the Barkers had found him friendly and courteous, a born musician who could play almost any instrument and who possessed a soulful tenor voice. But to them he was a foreigner. Also, he was almost as old as they were— not Janice's contemporary at all. Mama tried to talk to Janice about her plans, but Janice only laughed and said, "Now, Mama, you know you never could tell what I was apt to get into, could you?"

Papa always liked surprises, and a few days after Janice left he provided one. Even a little town like Tarpley was enjoying a business upsurge. Relief that the war had ended, optimism that this had been the war to end all wars, and confidence in a brighter future made business boom. Papa was working six days a week and the outlook was for a prosperous summer. In the spring Susan and Millie had complained about not having a piano so as to practice their music lessons, and Papa had wondered what was wrong with the organ. When they told him that nobody but nobody had an organ in the parlor anymore, he had continued to read the newspaper as if he hadn't even heard them, so no more was said on the subject. Then one Saturday Papa went to Asheville and came home in a big truck which was driven up to the house, and the driver deposited an upright Kimball piano for them. Mama was astonished and the girls were elated. "Now we can put the organ upstairs in the hall and the piano will make our parlor look like something to be proud of," said Millie.

"Papa, you're wonderful," Susan said as she embraced him.

Papa said nothing but the twinkle in his eye showed his pleasure.

14

Mama, as she said, was trying to "get her ducks in a row" before school started again. She had spent the morning canning soup mixture and had sat down on the porch to read and relax a little when Susan came in from the post office bringing two letters, one from Bob and one from Janice. Bob's note included the announcement of the birth of a son born the day before the letter was written. Mama knew that Bob and Lula were expecting and she knew that she would become a grandmother when the baby arrived, but she still felt a sense of shock. She didn't think she knew how to be a grandmother.

The news in Janice's letter, however, was like a bomb tossed in her lap. Both Janice and Pete had signed the letter that assured her that the course they had taken was to make it easier for her! Since they would be teaching in the same school again next year, they had decided to get married in Knoxville at the close of the summer school, thereby saving all the work and trouble of getting ready for a wedding. The chapel at the university was often used for weddings and they would be married there. Since Pete was a Catholic and wished it, they would go to a priest later and be married again. "Just think," wrote Janice, "won't it be fun to get married twice on the same day?" Mama really couldn't see anything funny about the whole situation, but she tried to remain calm and reminded herself that when a thing has happened in the family, whether she approved or not, she had to accept it and make the best of it. With Papa it was not that easy, however. He disliked the difference in their ages, he was suspicious of all "Eyetalians," and he had a strong prejudice against the Catholic Church. He was sincere in his concern for he was afraid Janice could not be happy with three such stumbling blocks in her way.

Bob's letter with the news of the arrival of the grandson was completely overshadowed by Janice's account of her plans. Her news called for action because the couple planned to spend the weekend with the Barkers on their way back to Pete's apartment in the little town where they would be teaching.

Susan defended Janice. "Can't you see, Mama, that she and Pete decided to get married this way to save you trouble? Don't you remember how hard everybody worked and had to be so involved for a whole month before Jane and Boyd's wedding?"

"It may be," Mama answered, "but I would have felt better if they had come home for the ceremony. Also, as I see it, the whole family is going to be quite as involved in this weekend visit."

Janice and Pete came driving up in a touring car, the back of which bulged with a conglomeration of musical instruments, books, papers, pots and pans, bedding, towels, and suitcases, while stuck in any available corner were articles almost forgotten, such as a pair of shoes, a comb stuck in a brush, and an umbrella. When Danny saw the car entering the driveway, his pride in having two brothers-in-law who owned cars took a tumble. He hadn't counted on the automobile so resembling a moving van.

Janice was her own irrepressible self—thrilled to be home, proud of being married, and perfectly sure that everybody would love Pete when they got acquainted with him. She chose to ignore the reserve with which Papa and Mama greeted Pete and kept up a lively chatter about their experiences in trying to get themselves and their belongings into the car to make the trip home.

Gradually Mama decided that the situation wasn't as bad as she had first thought. For one thing, Pete was not an "Eyetalian." Both his parents had been in their early thirties when they left Italy, and Pete had not arrived on the scene until after his parents had been

living in Baltimore for several years. He had brothers and sisters older and younger than he, so like Janice he was accustomed to a big family. Mama was also relieved to discover that Pete, even though in his late forties, had never been married. Papa, not very tactful at times, bluntly asked him why he had not married sooner and Pete had replied, "Well, I guess I had never met Janice until last year!"

When they had spent a day and night in Tarpley and continued on their way to school, Mama decided that the weekend was more pleasant than she had anticipated. She was still hurt that Janice had not wanted to come home to get married, but she had to agree that the way she and Pete chose was simpler and less expensive than a home wedding.

15

Tarpley College opened for another year the following week. Millie was beginning her senior year and had made for herself an enviable record. She was intelligent, a good mixer, dependable and ambitious. Susan was a sophomore. She was also intelligent, but she didn't seem particularly interested in her studies and said she was happy just to "get by." Danny was beginning seventh grade and Mama was back with her third grade students in the elementary school.

"How nice it is," said Mama, "for all of us to be back in our old routines where we can get down to steady work and not have some unexpected crisis hanging over us. I don't think I could take anything else right now! Two weddings and a grandbaby in less than a year!"

Soon after school started the County Fair was held. After the war in the Carolinas, county fairs had become very popular, and very few people in the area missed the opportunity of attending some or all of the events. On Friday afternoon Susan told Mama that she and her boyfriend Greg were going into Asheville to see the exhibits at the fair and "have a bite to eat" before they came home.

"I thought Millie wanted to go, too. Is she going with you?" Mama asked.

"We asked her and Greg's cousin to go with us, but she said she had some schoolwork she needed to do and declined," said Susan.

Danny, as all seventh graders in school, got a trip with his class to the fair. They had been given a half holiday from school and were chaperoned by their teachers. He came in soon after Susan had left and was so thrilled about what he had seen and done that he kept up a non-stop running conversation during supper.

When ten o'clock came and Susan had not returned, Mama began surreptitiously to keep an eye on the old clock on the mantel. It was not that she suspected anything wrong with the trip, but the morals of a young lady were very carefully supervised. Being out late at night with a beau always invited gossip, unless the couple had attended a concert or a public gathering that lasted late in the evening. Whatever the event, eleven o'clock was zero hour to be unaccounted for.

When the clock struck eleven, Mama said to Papa, who was dozing behind the newspaper, "Don't you think we had better do something—phone Greg's father or something?"

Millie hesitated a moment and then answered her mother, "I don't think you need to do that, Mama. Susan said she wasn't coming home tonight."

"What do you mean, and how do you know that?" asked Mama rather crossly.

"I guess you will blame me for this but I didn't see how I could do anything about it. Greg and Susan told me today they were not going to the fair. They went to Reverend Burton's house and got married. Then they planned to go to Knoxville for a honeymoon and will be home Monday."

"Ye gods and little fishes!" cried Mama. "Susan simply can't do that. She's not even eighteen! It won't be legal! Why in the name of all that's good and holy did she try such a scheme as that?"

"They had talked about it and they said they decided that since she would be eighteen next month she really is nearer eighteen than seventeen, so they were to put her age down as eighteen. She said she didn't want any bother about a wedding and Greg didn't either, especially since his mother has been dead so short a time. Susan meant well, Mama. I'm sure she wanted to make things easier on you. She said you didn't need any extra work and worry of any kind just now."

"Well, it's nice of you, Millie, to try to smooth things over, but you needn't trouble yourself. I know very well that Susan wasn't thinking of me nor was she worrying about my having extra work to do. I was concerned because she didn't take more interest in her schoolwork, but it never entered my head that she might be planning to get married now. Of course, I'm not happy about it. I wanted her to finish school for her sake no matter who she was going to marry later. Greg has been just sort of a fixture for the last couple of years around her, and we all like him, but I thought it was just a school boy and girl affair that might be broken off any moment."

"Well, Cora," said Papa. "I've told you that the more children a body has the more trouble they can bring you when they grow up."

"Sure, but I notice you didn't put into practice what you preach," was Mama's final shot.

The newlyweds arrived Sunday afternoon, a bit nervous and not quite sure of being welcomed. When they were invited to stay for supper they accepted eagerly. Conversation was general for a time and no mention was made of there having been a change in their relationship.

Finally Greg got up the courage to say that they meant no disrespect to their elders in taking things into their own hands as they had, but circumstances had changed their original plans. At first they meant to wait until Susan had finished school, but then his mother had become ill and some months later died. That left Greg and his father at home alone on the farm. Being an only child, Greg felt he must stay with his father, and he was sure Papa and Mama could see that they both needed somebody to help them. Susan agreed to leave school and to marry him, but she said she thought the easiest way to do it was to keep their plans a secret because she knew neither of her parents would approve of such an early marriage. "Mercy on us," thought Mama, "how did they think springing a surprise like this would make it easier on anybody?"

Mama said to Greg, "I thought you were planning to go to State College and study agriculture."

"Yes, mama, I was," Greg replied, "but I've decided that I can learn as much actually farming as I could get out of books and theories because I'd never know if these would work until I tried them on the land anyway."

"Under the circumstances, there is nothing left for us to say or do," said Mama, "except to wish you both good luck and to hope that Susan can learn to be a farmer's wife."

Both Greg and Susan seemed relieved that Papa and Mama were not going to make a scene.

Monday morning came and with it the rush to get everybody off to his particular task—Papa to work, Millie with her books slung across her shoulder to make an eight o'clock class, and Danny racing away to be sure he would not be tardy. Mama was not finding it easy to follow her own philosophy, "When a thing has happened in your family, you have to accept it and make the best of it," and she was woolgathering. She found the elopement to be unnecessary and was humiliated by it. She forced herself to get her materials together so she wouldn't be late for school, but she was finding it hard to be calm, and her naturally optimistic outlook seemed to have deserted her.

16

Seated at the table one evening soon after Susan's departure, Danny remarked, "This table looks too big for just four people. Maybe we'd better cut off one end of it."

"Don't let that bother you, son. They'll be coming back, and with the extra in-laws, we might end up needing an extension," said Mama.

In a few days Mama realized that she was acting like a child by nursing her own disappointment about the elopement, and while she brooded over that, there were many things she was neglecting. It occurred to her that Millie was rather lost without Susan. They had been together all their lives, always sharing the same room, even after the older children had left home and there was plenty of room to spare. Mama knew that she must be companionable to Millie and see that she was not left alone too much.

An event which created a lot of interest among Tarpley College students was the intercollegiate debate which took place every autumn. Some current national issue was chosen as the subject of the debate, and the pros and cons were argued by Tarpley College and a visiting school. The affair, which caused keen rivalry, was open to the public and was well attended. One day Millie came home with the news that she had been chosen as one of the debaters. While Millie was pleased to have been selected, Mama was elated. That meant that three of her children had represented the school in the debate. Mary, back in 1910, had the subject, "Resolved: that the United States should adopt a graduated income tax." When Jane was a senior in 1913, she had argued that women should be given the right to vote. And now Millie was going to try.

There was a great deal of controversy among colleges and universities about the ethical or legal right of the athletic department to give scholarships as a drawing card to get special athletes to attend these schools. Millie and her partner in debate had the negative side. She said she was sure they could win the decision, but it wouldn't make any difference if they did.

"What do you mean by that?" asked Mama.

"You know how it is," said Millie, "people are so sports-minded these days and the alumni of these schools are so keen on having their alma maters win that they would be willing to use any means to lure the best athletes to their schools."

Mama attended the debate anyway, and was pleased that Millie's side won, whether or not it would make any difference.

The days slipped by and the holidays were approaching. Mama got a letter from Jane telling her that she was not feeling up to par and had been advised by the doctor not to make a long automobile trip. Mama knew the rest—it only confirmed what she had been suspecting. She counted up the number of people she was expecting for Christmas dinner and arrived at nine. "Danny should be pleased," she thought, "for the table will be full again."

A few days later Greg and Susan dropped in. They had been to town shopping and were full of excitement as well as loaded down with bundles. They had come, Susan said, to invite the family to have Christmas dinner with them.

Mama said, "That's ever so kind of you children, but how could Susan take care of that many people? She has never tried to fix a meal all by herself for nine people in her whole life, I know."

"I might help her a little bit," said Greg, "but we are planning to do it and we expect you to come."

"And Mama," continued Susan, "you are not to bring anything— not anything! I know you—you'll be trying to bring some fresh sausage, or bake the turkey for us, or bring one of your fruit cakes, but this time that's out—all of it."

The Simmons farm was situated just outside the town limits of Tarpley, where the land lay in the fertile valley of Jarvis Creek. The homestead was a two-story clapboard house with a porch across the front both up and downstairs. A hallway ran through the center of the house with rooms opening on either side of it. Directly behind the hall was an ell in which were located the kitchen, pantry, back porch and a "shed room." The last room was a storage place for tools as well as the place where firewood was stacked for winter use. There was nothing pretentious about the house but it was well built and had been kept in good repair. Mrs. Simmons had loved flowers, and her boxwoods, lilacs, iris borders, holly, and dogwoods were lovely reminders of her work.

Greg and Susan, with a little help from Millie, served dinner just as if they were experienced hands. When everyone had done full justice to the meal, they gathered in the parlor where the air was fragrant with the smell of pine and cedar.

After the dominoes and carol singing the group rose to go, and Mama told her hosts it had been a lovely occasion. But she thought to herself, "Why can't pleasures like this last? Why does time march on so relentlessly so that even by tomorrow things may be changed?"

At home and in bed, Mama's thoughts continued. "And how does anyone know what is best to strive for? Here are two children, both of whom decided to quit school, elected to elope, concluded they could manage a farm—Susan without any experience—and have proceeded to try out their theories which, so far, seem to be working. Greg acts as if everything is as it should be. Susan's inexperience doesn't bother him, even if he does say there are two things she won't do— milk a cow and kill a chicken. Susan did look tired tonight, but she also looked happy. It's probably a good thing she doesn't know just what sort of a job she has undertaken. Dear Lord, help her be strong enough so that she won't lose her youth, her vitality, and her good looks before she is even grown up."

17

By the end of the first week in January, all the Barkers were back at their posts, ready to start another year. In the early 1920's drastic changes were taking place in the Asheville area. More tourists came. Before the war the Carolina mountains had drawn visitors because of the climate and scenery, but now it seemed that many who had formerly thought of the region as a summer vacation attraction were beginning to consider it as a possible year-round home. Land values mushroomed and there was a building boom in progress. Real estate dealers were having a field day. Even a small town like Tarpley was having new developments like Carson's Acres, Willow Heights, and Seven Oaks.

A famous author built a home and came to Seven Oaks to live. He gave as his reason the year-round climate. It was far enough south to escape the long sieges of bitter winter weather and far enough north to miss the unbearable sticky sweltering summer heat of the deep South. He said he found it to be the nearest to an ideal year-round climate.

Papa came home with the news that he had been approached by an agent who offered to buy the Tarpley house and the lots surrounding it.

"What would we do if you sold it, Papa?" asked Danny. "This is home."

Mama was writing her "duty" letters that night and she mentioned to Mary that Papa had been approached about selling the house. She passed it on as a matter of family news and thought little about it. But almost by return mail Mary answered, "I think it would be a very wise move to make. If Papa can get a good price for the place, why not sell it? I've written Nate and told him about the offer and I expect that he will want to come home next weekend with me to talk about this."

Mary, the spokesman and probably the instigator of the plan, had it figured out this way: they could sell the Tarpley property, take the money, and build a new house at the Briar Patch. There seemed to be no special reason to stay in town now that Millie would be graduating in May and Danny, being a boy, could make the two miles from the farm to the school without too much trouble. Besides, by the time he was old enough to drive, they would be able to get a T model.

Papa said that if they did move out to the Briar Patch he wanted to divide the land. Since there were forty-five acres there, he could reserve five acres for him and Mama and give each child five acres. "It isn't much," he said laughingly, "when you compare it to George Vanderbilt's four thousand acres and him with just one child to inherit it!"

"You should have thought about that and selected a shipping mogul for your grandfather instead of a circuit-riding Methodist preacher," quipped Nate.

Mary, Nate, Millie, and Danny were to have their plots designated and their deeds drawn up, but they asked that these be situated around the homestead. If any of the four children not present wanted money instead of land, Mary and Nate offered to help buy the land from them.

Word of the land division was sent to the other children. Bob immediately asked for the money. Susan said that since Greg didn't need any more land, she'd like to have a nest egg of her own. Jane and Janice both thought they might like to have a summer home built on their plots some day so a deed was all they wanted.

It didn't seem possible that people could be as busy as the Barker family that spring and summer. The house and land were duly sold, the Barkers to have an extension of six months before giving up possession of the house. The construction company for whom Papa worked was to build the new house, but they all knew they would be racing against a deadline to select the plans, get the building materials assembled, and complete the house in the allotted time.

The new house would not have any more room than the old one they were leaving, but it would be more convenient. There would be electric lights and a Holland furnace, the kind with one big register in the middle of the hall floor—a system which a great many people thought quite unnessary. The wide hall through the center of the house so popular in older homes was done away with. From the front entrance one walked into a large living room. A dining room separated from the living room by French doors extended across the front of the house. Behind the living room a narrow hall ran to the back and opened onto a small porch. On one side of the hall were two bedrooms with a bath between them. On the other was a breakfast nook, a kitchen, a pantry, and the back porch. In the hall a stairway led to the upper floor, where there was another bath and three bedrooms, each with its own closet space.

Mama had her moments of misgiving about the whole affair. There was so much bone weariness attached to moving. And there was also a big gap between a house on paper and the finished product. Maybe the family would not be as happy on the farm and away from their familiar associations in the town. "But," she concluded, "we mortals are like that—we're never satisfied with things as they are and we're always wanting something different from what we've got."

Commencement time came and Millie received her diploma. "Aren't you thrilled to be graduating, Millie?" Mama asked. "Just what did you think about when you walked across the stage to get your diploma?"

"Mostly I wondered if I could make it across without stumbling," Millie replied. "You know it was pretty dark back stage. Next I was sorry for the spectators who had to sit and see a hundred people dressed just alike file across the stage one at a time just to pick up a piece of paper and shake hands with the president. But I'm happy to be out of school even if it reminds me of our new house. People keep saying how wonderful it will be to have a new house. They don't count the time or take into consideration the labor that will have to be put out in making the move. My getting out of school is like that, too. Friends speak as if graduating were a grand finale and the end of the rainbow when it really is like an invisible presence saying, 'Now you're finished; get out and see what you can do for yourself.' "

Moving day arrived and Mama could not help contrasting it with the move from Swannanoa eighteen years ago. She decided that the confusion was the same, but trucks transported their possessions this time and accomplished in a few hours what had taken more than a whole day to do back then.

The site of the new house was a knoll in a grove of oak, poplar, and hickory trees, with a profusion of dogwoods growing among them, refusing to be choked out even through they were small. The house, being built on this high spot, afforded a magnificent view of the surrounding countryside and of the mountains beyond.

As had been expected, the inside work on the new house was not completed when they had to leave their old home. The bathroom fixtures upstairs were not installed, the back porch was not yet screen-ed, the kitchen cabinets were not in place, and a host of other small details remained to be looked after. The family didn't seem to mind very much though. These deficiencies were overshadowed by their pride in a new home that they had seen grow, as Danny said, "from a hole in the ground."

The summer wore on and another problem still had to be settled. Mama had deliberately put off thinking of school and had concen-trated on getting a schedule worked out for the family that they could live with. However, when she came face to face with their situation, she realized that this house would neer be a proper home unless some-one stayed eternally on the job until it was finished. Also she ad-mitted to herself that she doubted her ability to walk three miles a day, work eight hours at school, then have the energy enough at her age to come home and be able to turn herself into a magician who could cook and clean for the family. She had wanted a new house and she was proud of it, but in acquiring it she had forfeited her place as a teacher. "Oh well," she sighed, "life is like that. You get one thing you have been working for and then find out you have to give up something else in order to do it."

Mama thought her living room was just right. There was a red brick mantel and an open fireplace at one end of it, flanked on either side by built-in bookcases. She pointed out to the family that their books were not just alike in rows on shelves like some libraries in fine homes, but these were like old friends, acquired over the years to be read rather than used as decorative items. Susan, who was an artist with the needle, had done a really professional job on the curtains she had made. Mary had bought a nine by fifteen Wilton rug, which looked ever so nice on the floor that had been treated with orange shellac and waxed until it shone.

Papa had built a small barn and they got a cow. Mama thought it a luxury to have their own butter and milk again, but she also thought the chores were tedious and never ending. She remembered old Uncle Bill with special gratitude as she thought of his kindly help back in the days when she and Papa were newlyweds. Even now she hated to admit how little she had known about managing a house back then.

18

Early in September Mama went to see Jane and Boyd. One Friday night Boyd had telephoned to say that Jane had just delivered a baby boy. Jane had written earlier and asked Mama to come down and keep house while she was in the hospital and then stay a week or two after she and the baby came home.

Millie, who was at home teaching in the elementary school, could look after the family in Tarpley, and one Saturday morning she and Danny got out the horses and buggy and drove Mama to Tarpley. Mama and Millie then caught the interurban to Asheville. At Pack Square they transferred to the streetcar that took them to the depot. Millie stayed with Mama until she was seated on the train.

The train was not crowded so Mama did not have to share her seat. She settled herself, took off her hat, leaned her head back, and closed her eyes. She had always thought the train was a comfortable way to travel—it was so restful to sit in the plush seat and not even have to think. She was not accustomed to being still very long during the daytime, and soon after the train began its rhythmic journey, she was soundly sleeping.

She had been a little anxious, wondering just what she would do if there was no one to meet her when she got off the train. But she need not have worried, for even from the window she spotted Boyd's tall figure in the crowd.

He was more talkative than usual as they drove out to Morgan Hill. Jane was doing fine, he said, but she was mighty anxious to get home. At the hospital they only allowed her to have the baby every four hours at feeding time and once or twice the little tyke was brought in and she could tell he had been crying for a long time. Jane said if she could have him with her, he wouldn't do that.

"Isn't it strange how having a baby of your own changes your viewpoint?" Mama asked. "You hear other people talk about a baby crying and they tell you it develops a child's lungs and does him no harm. Maybe so, but if that baby is yours, it's a different story. You want to know why he cries and if there isn't something you can do to comfort him."

"Everybody who has seen the baby tells me he is an especially fine looking youngster, and of course I believe every word they say," said Boyd.

Jane had written her parents during the summer telling about the house they were building. They had moved into it a couple of months before the baby was due. Mama was naturally very interested and curious to see the place. She couldn't help comparing it to her new house, but was visibly impressed with what she saw. The rooms were spacious and the walk-in closets seemed huge. There was a butler's pantry as well as a kitchen pantry, and in the former was an honest-to-goodness electric refrigerator. You didn't have to buy ice for it, since it made its own and there was no drainage from it. Somewhere Mama had read that the ice the refrigerator manufactured might not be safe to put in tea or other cold drinks, but she hoped that was not the case. The next marvel to catch her attention was the new electric stove. It was like a table with four coiled burners on the left side and an oven taking up all the space on the right. It was hard for her to imagine that if you wanted to cook, you just turned a button and the heat came on. Mama knew too well the tedium and sometimes the frustration on cold mornings of shaking down ashes, building a fire, and then waiting for the stove to get hot enough to bake biscuits.

Of course, she was delighted that Boyd and Jane could have a place like this one, and she rejoiced with them, but her unspoken thoughts were, "I do hope these children haven't gone too deeply in debt to get all this. Young people nowadays don't seem to mind owing money and they believe good times are here to stay. I only hope they will be able to stem the tide if and when it does turn."

A few days later, Jane and the baby came home and immediately everything centered around the new member of the family. Since he had not yet been named, the three grown-ups discussed that first. "I suppose he is to be a junior," said Mama.

"No ma'am," said Boyd decisively. "He doesn't need my name and I heartily dislike hearing a child called "Junior." I would personally like to name him for my father, but I'd not give him Dad's full name so he would be John Doe the second or third or whatever. He needs a title of his own."

Jane said, "In that case, why don't we call him Stanley Joseph Brooks? He wouldn't be a junior and he would have one of the names of both of his grandfathers."

"How would you like that, Mama?" asked Boyd.

"I couldn't think of a better name," she answered. "But I really had not thought much about names for grandchildren. I have only one real request to make. If you ever have a daughter, don't call her Cora."

"You needn't worry," said Jane. "I love you dearly, Mama, but you've never seemed like 'Cora' to me, and I wouldn't inflict that name on a little girl myself."

And laughing, they closed the subject.

Old Aunt Rose called herself a nurse and she made her living by spending a month or two in the homes of mothers with new babies "to help get them started off right," she said. Boyd had engaged her to stay with Jane, and she came in a few days before Mama was to return home. Aunt Rose showed plainly that she was not enthusiastic about having another woman around who might question her authority. Mama, quick to sense the situation and knowing that Jane needed Aunt Rose, deliberately set about to make friends with the old woman and to avoid any arguments about the care of the new baby.

Boyd, being the youngest child of his parents, knew very little about new babies, and he seemed all too satisfied for someone else to look after the child. That to Mama was much better than if he had felt it his privilege and duty to dictate to others how and what should be done for the child or what others should do for him.

When Mama left she told Jane that things would get easier as time went on, and she was sure Jane would get along fine.

"I hope so," said Jane. "But I never was so scared nor felt so helpless in my life as I do right now."

19

Back at home, Mama had the sensation of being catapulted headlong into a beehive of activity. The apple crop had been gathered and Papa was storing the sound ones for winter use. There were also pumpkins and cabbages to be stored. A little way behind the new house, the hill dropped sharply and formed a bank. Papa dug a six-foot cubicle from this bank, put a roof over the top, made a framework for the open side, and hung a solid wooden door across the front. He believed the thick, solid, earthen-sided root cellar would keep produce from freezing even in the coldest weather.

Mama had her work cut out for her, too. From the apples she made apple butter and applesauce, which she then canned. From the cores and peelings she made several jars of the rich, red apple jelly they all loved. With all the work that the farm required, Mama wished she had some paid help, but the Barkers had always been "do-it-yourselfers."

When the Carolinas were being settled, slave owners did not come to the mountain section, for people in the hills didn't farm on the scale to make slave ownership profitable. In all of Tarpley, almost fifty years after the War Between the States, there were no more than a half-dozen families who had elected to settle on what was called "Chocolate Hill" in the south part of town. Most of these residents worked as domestics or handymen, but the Barkers had not hired any outside help since old Aunt Althea had come to do the wash when the children were little.

Mama could especially have used some help at Christmastime, when the whole family was there for the first celebration in the new house. Delightful stories are written about the joys of a Christmas homecoming when all the family members assemble without any problems and when peace and good will permeate the atmosphere. It sounds idyllic, but in these descriptions the author usually has all the food and hosting preparations done to a turn and served at the right moment, as though someone waved a magic wand and presto—everything was all finished and ready to serve.

Mama knew better. She knew what had to be done and she also knew who would have to do the biggest part of the work. Susan was, however, a lifesaver to her. She volunteered to make the dessert and to "sleep" the overflow crowd at her house on Christmas Eve.

Christmas came and went with lightning speed. It was a lot of work but after it was over Mama enjoyed it in retrospect. Could there ever have been a family with so many occupations? There was a band director, a garage mechanic, a hotel clerk, a chain store executive, a teacher, a farmer, and a home demonstration agent. Could so many people with such diverse occupations ever have enough in common to enjoy their association as a family group? "Only time will tell," Mama thought.

A few days after the holiday was over, Mama answered the Barker ring on the telephone, which was two longs and one short. It was Susan, asking to speak to Millie. When Mama told her that she had not yet come from school, Susan said she wanted to ask Millie to spend the night with her. Mama pointed out that it was a cold day for such a long walk, but Susan told her that Greg had to go into town and could pick her up. "Do tell her to be sure to come," said Susan.

Mama had been a bit suspicious about Susan at Christmas and she was pretty sure she knew what her urgency was to see Millie. More than likely Susan was "in the family way." Mama had a hard time admitting it to herself, but she was a bit jealous that Susan was turning to Millie instead of her own mother. "Oh well," thought Mama, "they do belong to another generation from me, and I guess they think I don't know where babies come from."

When Millie came home the next day she gave Mama an account of her visit with Susan. "When I first got there, I thought she was deathly ill or at least had suffered a nervous breakdown, but after a couple of hours she perked up and acted very much like her old self. She finally told me that she was expecting and that was what made her feel so bad. I feel sorry for her, Mama. She has an awful lot of hard work to do, and also being the only woman around I know she gets lonesome at times."

"Yes, I know," Mama said. "At eighteen she thought she was grown-up and very self-sufficient. Now she will have to live and act like a grown woman. I'm sorry she is so miserable, but unless there is some complication we don't know about, she will survive and probably be none the worse for her ordeal. As I've said before, experience is a great school."

Not only did Susan survive the birth of healthy baby girl in

71

September of that year, but in exactly eighteen months she had a second child, this time a boy, lusty and vocal and determined to make himself heard. Mama and Millie were both on hand to help with the housework on both occasions, and Susan decided she liked being a mother just as much as she liked being a farmer's wife.

News from Bob in the following week included the announcement of another expected increase in his family, and before that fact was fully digested, Jane wrote that little Stan was soon to have a brother or sister. The letters caused Millie to remark,"At this time the Barkers seem to be going in for mass production."

"Sakes alive, Millie, how you do talk," said Mama. "But," she continued, "I'm bewildered myself. I grew up expecting to get married and have as many children as the Lord saw fit to send. I was so naive it never occurred to me to try to limit my family, and yet after two pregnancies, Susan loudly declares she's not going to have any more children. Most young couples nowadays seem to share Susan and Greg's ideas about limiting families. Who could believe that people's thinking could undergo such a change in a little over thirty years? I thought if Papa and I could see that all of you got an education, everything else would fall into place. You would all be a tight little group having the same ambitions and plans I had. I thought we would be able to work as a unit and come what may put up a solid front to the world! So what is the result to date? Some of you graduated, some didn't, but as soon as you finished school or decided you were grown, you scattered, each one in a different direction. It's only when they're little that children behave as their parents expect them to."

20

The 1920's had been kind to Boyd and Jane. Their attractive new home was a noted addition to Morgan Hill, and they were duly proud of it. The premises were showing marked improvement, for Jane, with her love for flowers and her fondness for the outdoors, was soon getting shrubbery planted and flower borders in place. There was also a space in the back for a kitchen garden. Boyd admitted that he didn't like to get his hands dirty, but if Jane would manage he'd see she had help for the heavy work. He was as good as his word, and soon an old colored man was spending four days a week working on the grounds.

There seemed to be a mood of optimism everywhere. The war was over, money was plentiful, life-styles were changing, and a religious sect predicted that the end of the world was near. Boyd received another promotion, becoming manager for a group of stores in the area. Since this job meant traveling a good deal, the company furnished him a car, which in turn gave Jane the use of the family car. She was as busy as Boyd and, as she said, her hours were longer than his. Boyd's mother was an unusually good cook, a thrifty manager, and a meticulous housekeeper. Jane felt her own inadequacy compared to that of her mother-in-law, and she was sometimes very discouraged when she baked a cake that fell in the middle or let the fried chicken burn. Teaching school, for her, had been lots easier.

One day when Boyd came home for lunch, they were eating on the screened porch just off the dining room. Jane brought out some rolls, piping hot from the oven. Stan reached for one and immediately flung it away from him. "Why did you do that, son?" asked Boyd.

Stan looked solemnly at his daddy and replied, "Hot, too 'dan' hot."

With a wry grin on his face, Boyd looked at Jane. He was aware of the fact that she had cautioned him about using certain expressions before Stan and he had laughed at her, saying that Stan was too little to pay any attention to him. Now the tables were turned, and he was completely taken by surprise at his son's remark. He grinned sheepishly at Jane and said, "you're not saying anything, but your eyes tell me 'I told you so.' "

A day or so later Boyd noticed the spring on the outer door screen seemed to be sagging and discovered that the screws holding the spring had worked loose. He got some longer screws and some tools and set about to fix it. Moments later, hearing a howl and a commotion, Jane rushed to the door of the porch and asked the proverbial silly question, "Did you mash your finger?"

Boyd was standing there holding onto his thumb and balancing himself first on one foot and then the other. He glared at her and shouted, "Hallelujah! Darn! Heck fire and katoot!"

Then defensively and in an injured voice he said, "At least I hope you noticed I didn't curse this time."

"No, you didn't, Honey," said Jane. "But what I heard sounded like a pretty good imitation to me."

The next acquisition in the Brooks household was a cabinet radio. The loudspeaker was concealed in the console and there would be no more need for earphones and the unsightly and temperamental box on the library table. The radio thrilled and amazed Jane. How in the world could any such insignificant looking device pluck sounds from the air and bring them into your home? All the wonderful music and the news from all over the world made the world seem intimate and small. The house itself seemed more alive and there was added character to the atmosphere. Even the children were affected by it and wanted the radio turned on whenever they were in the house.

Boyd's work schedule was a demanding one and his days were full. Jane was surprised at the varied things he tried to promote— some new product for distribution, an appealing and different window display, or a seasonal advertising campaign for certain articles. In addition to these chores, he had to know in dollars and cents if these efforts were profitable as well as how each store was doing individually. Then there were board meetings, sales meetings, and sessions with the auditors.

Many of these affairs took place at night, and Boyd wanted Jane to go with him. They found a responsible middle-aged woman to stay with the children, since it was unthinkable to hire a teenage babysitter, and the two were constantly on the go. Also, a number of young couples had formed a square dance club and the Brooks were invited to join. Boyd enthusiastically said they'd be delighted. He had no qualms at all, but Jane was a little reluctant. She was pretty sure Mama and Papa would really not approve, but she reasoned, there actually didn't seem to be any harm in dancing, and wasn't that something she and Boyd would have to decide for themselves? The club was made up of a friendly lot of young couples and the square dancing was really fun, so for a few months these get-togethers were a pleasant diversion. Then Jane began to be a little uneasy.

Prohibition to these young people was an unjust law, one to be broken and ignored. They had no qualms about flouting it. The punch bowl was spiked and there were drinks for those who wanted them. By the time the party was over, there were always one or two individuals who had imbibed too freely.

One night when they were driving home Jane complained about the drinking and Boyd said, "Don't be a spoil sport. There's no harm in breaking that kind of law, and these fellows don't do any harm that a good night's sleep won't cure. The girls seem to enjoy the punch. How do you like it?"

"I don't drink it."

"All I can say is you are missing a lot. It would help you relax and you would have a whole lot more fun."

By the time Stan was in the second grade, his little sister Janet was in kindergarten. Jane was busier than ever, chauffeuring the children from one place to another, working as a grade mother, and contributing volunteer service as a club member. She thought she would have more time when the children were in school, but it seemed that the reverse was true.

People no longer spent weekends at home. The whole country was on wheels, and treks to the mountains or the beach were becoming the accepted way of life. Jane remembered once back at home their whole family had gone visiting for a few days. Someone had asked Mama if she had enjoyed the vacation.

"Oh, yes, I did enjoy it," Mama said.

"What was the nicest thing about it?"

"The best of all was getting back home so I could rest from the trip," Mama replied.

Monday morning often found Jane feeling just as Mama had, but somehow the hectic pace went on into the next week just the same. The Square Dance Club had become The Cotillion, with an increased membership and an enlarged program. Boyd loved dancing and made every possible effort to be present at every meeting. He wanted Jane to have a new dress for every banquet, which prompted Jane to say,

"It's a funny world. I always thought it was the women who wanted fine clothes to wear and the men who resented the money spent on what they considered their wives' extravagance, but with our family it seems to be the other way around."

Soon, however, the club became a real source of anxiety for Jane. She felt completely helpless to cope with the situation that confronted her. This feeling was aggravated by the fact that she had no one in whom she could confide or with whom she could discuss the problem. Certainly she could not discuss the matter with Boyd, for when she tried to caution him or talk with him about drinking, they always somehow ended up in an argument with no solution and with their convictions farther apart than ever.

Jane didn't know where Boyd got his supply, but she realized that legal or not he always had a drink available. She also knew that he was mighty apt to take at least a little every day. Some people argued that if a supply was kept at home and cocktails were served openly, men would not sneak around to buy liquor and drink too much. Jane wasn't so sure that was the solution.

At the annual club banquet, Boyd was unsteady on his feet by the time they started home. They made it safely to the garage, but Jane was unnerved and tense. She realized that in spite of all his boasting that "he knew when to stop," poor Boyd was only fooling himself.

21

That December Jane and Boyd decided that since it was probably the last Christmas the children would really enjoy having a visit from Santa, they should make special plans for the visit of the jolly old man. They invited Boyd's family to dinner and began early to buy presents for the children and stashing them in Boyd's office, safe from prying eyes.

On Christmas Eve, when Stanley and Janet were finally in bed, Boyd brought the packages into the living room to put them under the tree. Just as they had begun to arrange the gifts, the telephone rang. It was a friend of Boyd's asking him to come to town to meet a war buddy of theirs who was in town for the holidays. "I won't be gone long," he told Jane as he went out.

Jane busied herself for a time putting last minute touches to the table, checking on the turkey, which was already in the oven, and mixing a salad. She could not help watching the clock, and as time dragged on her apprehension grew.

Shortly after one o'clock she heard the front door open and footsteps in the hall. There were three men, one on either side of Boyd, holding him up. The men told Jane that they were happy to meet Boyd's wife, that they had been having a little party talking about their days in France, and that Boyd had had "a little too much" so they thought they had better see him home.

At that moment a flash of recognition seemed to come to Boyd. He looked up at Jane with attempted bravado and said, "Hi, Toots!"

"Take him into the den," directed Jane, as she opened the door for them to enter. When she indicated the couch to place him on, one of the men told her they would take him to the bedroom and undress him for her, but she thanked him and told him she could manage herself.

After wishing her a Merry Christmas several times over, the two men left. If Jane had been describing their departure in mountain dialect, she would have said they "snuck out."

Bone tired, hurt, and humiliated, she stood for a long time looking at her sleeping husband and then went to work. She took a flashlight and made several trips to the garage to bring in the remaining packages for the tree and stockings. She tore off the outside wrappings in the kitchen, took the gifts into the living room, and placed Stan's on one side of the chimney and Janet's on the other. In the stockings on either side of the mantel, she put fruit, candy, and small gifts.

As Jane was tidying up the kitchen she speculated: she could have a crying binge and develop a sick headache, or she could call Boyd's family and say he had come down with a virus, or she could go to bed, try to get an hour or two of sleep, and go ahead with the plans as if nothing had happened. By gum, that's what she would do! She angrily brushed away the tears that kept coming into her eyes.

As she was going to bed she checked in the den to see about Boyd. Snoring heavily, he lay exactly as they had placed him. She took off his shoes, put a pillow under his head, and threw a blanket over him. The air seemed stuffy to her, so she raised a window. Then she closed the door and went to bed.

As she had expected, she heard the children's excited voices before six o'clock on Christmas morning. Going hurriedly into the living room, she toned down the radio, cautioned the children about making too much noise because Daddy had a headache, and shared with them their delight in what Santa Claus had brought.

After fixing breakfast for the children, she and the maid stayed busy the rest of the morning preparing dinner. The guests arrived promptly and sat down at the table soon after. Jane had debated about whether to lay a place for Boyd or not, but she quickly realized that since the table was round there wouldn't be a gap anyhow. Everyone expressed sympathy and disappointment because Boyd was not feeling well, but Jane felt that Boyd's family knew what had happened and were gallantly trying to help her make the best of it. It would always be a day of torture for her to remember.

By the time the guests left and general clutter surrounding the tree had been cleared away, the children came in from outside declaring they were hungry. Stan looked a little worse for wear, with a muddy coat, scratches on his legs, and torn stockings. "I fell a few times," he admitted, "but pretty soon I'm going to get the hang of my new bike and will be able to ride it."

While they were in the kitchen having a snack, Boyd came in, fresh from a bath, clad in his robe and slippers, his hair neatly combed, and no stubble showing on his chin. He sat down to drink a cup of black coffee. The children greeted him warmly, glad that his headache was gone. They insisted that he come see what Santa had left them and open his own packages.

When Stan and Janet had gone to bed, Boyd said, "Jane, I can't begin to tell you how terrible I feel about this. I simply don't know how it happened. The boys were there recalling things we did in France, and the bottle was being passed around although I didn't think I was drinking much. Then all at once everything was blank and that's the last thing I remember. That's all there was to it."

"No, it wasn't all! We were going to work on the dinner and play Santa Claus, remember?"

"Don't be cross, Jane. I've told you already that I feel too awful for words, but don't you think I need a little understanding?"

"I do understand," Jane said tartly. "I understand that you need a swift kick in the pants. I've been awake and at work almost all the time you have slept, I'm dead tired and am going to bed. And I never expect to have another Christmas party again, no matter how long I live."

22

In the days that followed Boyd worked exhaustingly long hours. He also worked hard at repairing the rift in his family. He was especially agreeable to the children, playing games with them and taking them on outings. One day they all went up to Charlotte to see a new kind of picture show. It had sound as well as a picture and they were all thrilled at Al Jolson's singing.

Boyd told Jane in all seriousness that he was going to stop drinking. He knew he would never allow himself to repeat the Christmas Eve experience, and he would make it up somehow. Being a self-satisfied male, he couldn't understand her lack of response to his declarations. He had told her how sorry he was, hadn't he? He had made her a solemn promise, hadn't he? And he was going to do something especially nice for her, wasn't he? After all that, why couldn't she forgive and forget so things could be as they were before?

Jane couldn't understand how she could ever feel normal again after the Christmas ordeal, but she kept herself busy. While she had a washing machine, dryers were a thing of the future, and she often had to dry the children's clothes over the radiator during the dreary, rainy January. She attended a mission study course at the church and helped with a P.T.A. bake sale. On all sides she heard complaints of inflation and rising prices. Some commentators on the radio predicted a stock market crash, while others declared such a thing couldn't happen.

A letter from Mama brought the distressing news that Janice was ill and had been ill for several weeks. Doctors had advised surgery. Pete, having lived in a bachelor's apartment for years, could look after himself, but eighteen-month-old Marinella must be provided for. Mama had told the Lavorinis to bring the baby to Tarpley while her mother was in the hospital.

The next letter brought the news that a mastectomy had been performed. Janice had stood the operation well but was recuperating slowly. The baby was a happy little thing, inquisitive as a kitten, but completely adorable. When Danny was around she was his shadow, which so flattered him that they became great pals. She was learning to talk, and when Danny tried to get her to say her name she shortened it to "Nella." Immediately, the nickname replaced Marinella.

Jane knew that Janice was seriously ill and that her chances for a complete recovery would hang in the balance for months to come. She also thought Mama was too old to assume the responsibility of a young child. Boyd, sensing that Jane was worried about affairs at home, suggested that she take the children and spend a few days in Tarpley. They agreed that he would take them to the train on Tuesday and drive up on the weekend to bring them home.

Often sisters who have been separated for ten or more years, living in different states establishing their own families, find they have lost the feeling of closeness they shared as adolescents. This was not the case with Janice and Jane. The week was a glorious reunion for them, and Mama said it helped Janice more than any treatments she could have had, for Janice had been frightened and depressed because of her ordeals. When Jane came the sisters re-lived many of their girlhood experiences, laughed at their escapades, talked over their housekeeping problems, and had a wonderful time.

On Saturday morning Jane began to collect her children and belongings to make the trip home. She would have sworn that she did not believe in ESP and would have pooh-poohed the fact that one could have presentiments, but she felt a vague sense of uneasiness. When supper time came and Boyd had not appeared, her heart sank. A couple of hours later when he called her to explain that he had been delayed, she knew what she did not want to know.

At midnight, when the household was asleep with the exception of Mama and Jane, he arrived. He was still on his feet, but he was staggering, and his pathetic efforts to tell Mama he had been suffering from headaches lately made Jane feel sick inside. The next morning Jane was able to get Boyd awake enough to dress himself and come to the table. He could only drink coffee and nibble at his food, but the conversation went on as if nothing was out of kilter.

As soon as they left Tarpley, Jane insisted that she drive. Boyd was reluctant for her to do so, but finally he stopped the car, got into the back seat, made a pillow out of the suitcases, and was soon sleeping audibly. when they got back to Morgan Hill, Jane fed the children, helped them get a bath, located their paraphernalia for school the next day, and sent them off to bed. Boyd, still groggy, ate a little soup, stumbled into his room, and fell on the bed.

Jane put things right in the kitchen and went into her desk. She was tired, frustrated, uneasy about Janice, and disgusted and embarrassed by her husband. She had promised Mama that she would drop her a note that night, so she got pen and paper and began:

Dear Mama,

We got home about sunset and since everybody was tired, it did not take long to get through with the nightly chores. Janet and Stan said that the piece of cake you gave them was "good to the last crumb."

The house was steeped in silence. The only sound to be heard was the ticking of the clock in the hall. As Jane sat there she was suddenly overwhelmed with a longing to share her own feelings of helplessness and her anxiety for the days ahead. She wrote:

Mama, have you ever been afraid of your husband? Knowing Papa, of course you haven't! I don't mean really fearing physical violence, but being afraid, as I am, of what Boyd might do when he is under the influence and also for what might happen to him when he has reached the unconscious state.

Boyd has always argued that a person's individual freedom is unlawfully restricted if he is told he cannot take a drink. He says that if prohibition laws were repealed it would stop drunkenness—people would feel free to indulge moderately and no one would drink too much at a time.

I went along with that for a while because I didn't know what else to do, but gradually I had to realize that he was not able to stop at a few drinks and that he would not be quite sober when we were ready to leave a banquet or party. There's no need to go into all the details about how in the first stage everything to him is uproariously funny and he talks too much. Then he lapses into a sort of stupor, and following that, he goes out like a light that has suddenly been turned off. It takes twenty-four to thirty-six hours for Boyd to get over the effects of a bout and be on his feet again.

He has never yet admitted that he is helpless once he takes a drink, and after every binge he declares he will never

82

let it happen again, but of course he is the only one who believes that.

The tears had been falling as Jane wrote. Some even splashed onto the letter. Finally she stopped and sat looking vacantly around her. She would never mail this letter to her mother, but putting her dilemma into words had given her a certain sense of release and she felt refreshed for the moment.

After she read her letter over one more time, she tore it into small bits and put the pieces in the wastebasket. Then she took fresh paper and began again:

Dear Mama,

The trip home was uneventful and we arrived before dark. We had lots to talk about discussing the nice things that happened during our stay with you.

Thank Papa especially for the apples and vegetables he put in the car. We are going to have a good many feasts because of his generosity.

I do sincerely hope that Janice can continue to be optimistic and hold on to her hopeful outlook. What could happen if she has a recurrence of her trouble simply doesn't bear thinking about.

It is late and soon the Monday morning alarm will be sounding off, so I must close with love to all of you.

Jane

23

Through the summer Janice continued to improve and the baby, free to play outside, was happy as a lark. When the school term began, Pete came for them and they went back to their school.

One morning Papa went into Tarpley and noticed a crowd of people in the post office. There was an air of excitement in the crowd and people were pouring over the black headlines which announced that the New York Stock Market had crashed. Tarpley was excited by the news, although few citizens had any understanding of what had really happened or what effect such a calamity could have on local affairs. A neighbor jokingly said to Papa, "How do you suppose it feels to be a millionaire one day and wake up the next to find you are a pauper?"

"I wouldn't know," said Papa. "But it is sort of comforting to know you can't lose a million if you have never had it."

The upheaval did not seem to have any noticeable effect on the people of Tarpley for some time. Everybody talked about the crash, wondered how it could have happened, read conflicting opinions from newspaper editors as to what effect it would have on the country's economy, and were appalled by some of the tragedies that took place following the debacle. Then, after a few weeks, life went on as usual and the people turned their minds to local affairs.

It was not until the first part of the 1930's that a noticeable change came over Tarpley. Industrial plants began operating five and sometimes four days a week, teachers' salaries were reduced, farm surpluses could not be sold, and many people found themselves out of work.

Mama was confused by it all. How could the crash of the New York Stock Market have such a devastating effect on everyone in the country? She knew vaguely that rich people invested lots of money in stocks and bonds and that this procedure somehow brought them dividends. Then there were others who bought shares with the hope of selling them soon at a higher price and that was gambling. She was not just exactly sure who was the investor and who was the gambler.

News from Pete and Janice put all thoughts of material matters out of Mama's mind, however, for Janice had been ill again and her doctors had recommended further surgery. The news came as a double blow this time, since Janice had seemed so well for nearly four years. Everybody in the family had been confident she would not have any recurrence of her trouble.

Again Janice returned to Tarpley for the summer. She was in the hospital in Asheville for two weeks, when a hysterectomy was performed. Although she was very weak, there had been no complications and the doctors spoke hopefully of the chances for recovery.

In spite of the shadow hanging over the household, it was a happy summer. Papa's age and rheumatism made it necessary of him to give up his "public work" as he called it, and he spent his time with his truck farming and gardening. All of the other children were either working or away at summer school, so Mama had the housework to do herself, but some of the children came home every weekend, and the house was filled with pleasant activity.

Toward the end of the summer Janice, Pete, and Nella got ready to go back to Tennessee. When the family had driven off, Mama and Papa went back into the kitchen to have a cup of coffee. Both wanted to talk, but neither knew how to express the concern they felt or the uneasiness which they shared.

"I don't think she is as much better as she tries to pretend," Papa said.

"Yes, I know, but I'm still glad for every day she can live feeling hopeful," said Mama. "I wish I had her optimism. I wonder why so useful a person and one so young should be the victim of such a horrible disease. The doctors themselves are about as helpless as we are, it seems."

The specter of Janice's illness stayed with them. Even on days when they didn't discuss her condition at all, both knew it was uppermost in their minds.

One day Mama got a letter from Millie. She had spent the summer in New York City studying at Columbia University, working, as Mary had done, on a master's degree in education. Mama was eagerly looking forward to Millie's return, for she had missed her companionship. The letter was a blow. Millie had been offered a teaching position in a school close to New York City. The pay scale was better than that in North Carolina, and she was sure they would be as happy as she was with her "advancement" as she called it.

Mama read the letter over several times as if she couldn't quite take in what was said. Then she looked around at her beloved mountains. There was Pisgah wrapped in an early morning blue haze rising to the east of her, the long Hog Back range formed the skyline to the south of the valley where they lived, and on the west were the three tall peaks that rose behind the nearer hills and at this distance they seemed identical. Local people called them the Three Sisters. In this lovely setting how could anyone want to leave? Mama had made only one trip to the seacoast in her life. She had loved the sight of the ocean and enjoyed walking on the beach, but when that fine white sand began to get in the floors of the cottage, in their clothing, even in the towels and bedclothes, she was ready to go home. When she returned from any trip the very sight of these hills spelled home to her. They were like old friends, and she drew comfort and strength from them. Why should all but one of her children prefer going to some other place to make their homes?

As Papa said at supper time, they were back to where they had started. After forty years of marriage, all their children were away and the two of them rattled around the house like a couple of peas in a pod. Soon, however, they established a pattern that made them feel not quite so lonely. Papa liked to come in at night, turn on the radio, eat supper, read *The Asheville Citizen,* and then have a game of dominoes or checkers before bedtime.

Mama didn't really enjoy the games, but she went along with his wishes. If any of the children dropped in or if Danny came home for the weekend, Mama always took advantage of their willingness to play with Papa and she dropped out of the game. Papa, on the other hand, really enjoyed playing with Mama the most, partly because Papa was almost always the winner when she was his opponent. One night Mama had a new book she was so interested in that she tried to snatch a few lines of it when it wasn't her turn to play. Papa resented her inattention and scolded her soundly. She ought to know it wasn't possible to concentrate on the game and read at the same time, and it wasn't fair to her partner. So Mama laid aside her book and took up the challenge. She beat him soundly for the next three games. When they had finished playing, Papa remarked,"You're not that good, you just had a run of luck tonight."

The next day Jane phoned. It always made Mama a little nervous when she received a call—somehow she associated all long distance calls with trouble—but Jane had nothing but good news to report. Stan was back from a two-month bicycle tour of Europe in time to go back to Duke University and Janet was getting ready to go to Stanford.

"Do you mean," interrupted Mama, "Stanford University in California? Why, Jane, why ever in the world did she want to go so far from home? Won't it cost a fortune?"

"I wouldn't have chosen that school myself, but some time ago Boyd told Janet she could select her own school if she maintained the high average she was making. So, as he said, since she had kept her part of the bargain, it's up to him to keep his. But what's the news of Janice, Mama?"

"So far her letters have been cheerful, but she doesn't talk much about her condition. We keep hoping that everything will be all right, and we are looking forward to having her visit us for the summer."

"Of course you are, Mama, but you yourself need a rest. Remember what Boyd said about you years ago, that it's no wonder you and Papa haven't accumulated any money since you've run a free hotel for forty years."

"That's all right," said Mama. "I wouldn't know what to do with a lot of money and neither would Papa."

Only a fortnight after the conversation with Jane, Mama had a disturbing one with Pete. Janice was not any better. She was not even holding her own, but was losing ground steadily and suffering constantly. Pete's voice sounded faraway and sad.

In spite of the nagging uneasiness they had felt about the doctor's reports after Janice's last operation, the family, Mama included, had tried to see some evidence that a miracle might happen. But after Pete's call she knew this was the death knell to all their hopes. Janice was coming home for her last visit.

24

So the never to be forgotten summer began. Pete was troubled and apologetic. He seemed to feel that he was in some way remiss because he was unable to stay on his job, look after Nella, and give Janice the help she needed. There were staggering hospital and doctor bills accumulating, too. Both Papa and Mama assured him that they wanted Janice with them for the summer—or until she was better—they said, trying to be hopeful.

For a short time Janice did seem to improve. She was happy to be at home, to see other members of the family as well as friends who dropped in, and she tried desperately hard to be cheerful and interested in what went on around her.

If it had not been for the night ordeals, Mama herself would have been encouraged, but she knew Janice could never sleep at all without a sedative, and as soon as the effects of one dose wore off, she was awake and suffering. This was the heartbreaking part of it—the never-ceasing, intolerable pain which by its dogged persistence dragged her down, leaving those who loved her powerless to do anything to help her.

Mama was feeling the strain herself. Worn out with lack of sleep and physically weary from overwork, she sometimes wondered if she could last the day. When Mary came home for the weekend the first thing she did was to arrange for a nurse to come on duty every night for an eight-hour stint, but even so the going was hard and the whole family lived in a state of suspended anxiety.

As the weeks went by Janice weakened and her interest gradually narrowed to the four walls of the bedroom. She needed stronger opiates, and sometimes when she wakened from her drugged unconsciousness, she seemed disoriented and her memory was affected to the extent that she confused dates and events. Following a low point like this, for no apparent reason, there would come a few days when she was more comfortable. She would have a respite and be somewhat like her old self, interested in family affairs, planning for Nella to start school, enjoying the summer flowers.

But these interims came less and less often and were usually followed by a more terrible seizure when she would be conscious of nothing but the excruciating misery which engulfed her.

One day in the late summer, Janice roused from a drugged sleep and asked for Mama. She seemed entirely rational and very calm. Mama came into the room and stood by the bed rearranging the pillows.

"Mama," Janice said, "I know now that I am not going to get well."

"Oh, Janice, no!" burst from Mama involuntarily.

Janice continued, "I have been all over this many times and I have come through my Gethsemane. At first I was determined to get well, and for months I thought I would. Then when it came to me that I was losing ground, I was resentful. I asked myself, 'Why me? What have I done to bring this judgment on my head?' I have no answers for some of my questions, but I realize now that man is mortal and subject to all manner of diseases and afflictions and no one knows whose turn will be next. I believe in the eternal goodness of God and I do not believe that this terrible disease has anything to do with Him. It is one of the devastating evils of this imperfect world. Of course, I want to live. I want to see Nella grow up and for Pete and me to continue our music. But I simply cannot. The awful pain and the increasing helplessness have made it all impossible. And I'm so tired I will even be glad if the end comes soon."

Janice drifted off into a fitful sleep and Mama continued to stand by her bed, stroking Janice's forehead, mute, but herself dying a thousand deaths as she tried to accept the certain knowledge that Janice had just told her mother goodbye.

She died in September. The last week of her life was peaceful, for she lay in a coma and was oblivious to everything around her. Mama thought to herself that she would never have believed it possible to have a feeling of relief when a loved one was gone, but when she remembered the constant suffering Janice had to undergo this last summer, she was glad it was ended. Even though she knew life must go on, the grief and loneliness and a terrible vacancy would always be with her.

When Janice had been laid to rest in the Tarpley cemetery, Pete was back at work and Jane had taken Nella home with her, where she was to attend school. When Jane had asked Boyd about keeping Nella for the winter, he had said, "Sure, bring her along. You and I have been rattling around in this house ever since the children went off to school. Maybe Nella can put a little life into the place."

Tarpley people were neighborly and kind. They visited Mama, bringing her flowers and tempting delicacies, which she accepted gratefully. But she seemed to be in the grip of an overpowering lassitude from which she could not free herself. From lifelong habit she went about her household tasks. Automatically, she ate her meals and went to bed at night, but nothing registered with her. She felt as if she were living in a great void in which everything was blank except the grief and sorrow that Janice's death had brought.

It was in the late autumn before a sense of awareness began slowly to come back to her. She realized that in her own constant grieving she had neglected duties toward those around her. She must accept what had happened. Time, she knew, would help to heal the sorrow, but the loneliness and the ache, the ache would always be there.

25

When the new year came in it brought many changes to the Barker household. In December Mary had suffered a heart attack and was hospitalized for several weeks. The doctors strongly advised her not to try to continue the strenuous work she had been doing and recommended a complete rest for six months or so.

Papa and Mama wrote to Mary suggesting that she resign her position and come home to live with them. Papa, who was pushing eighty, said that when she got rested up he'd be glad to turn over the garden work to her. And Mama pointed out that it would be so nice for Papa to have someone to play dominoes with at night.

In a few weeks Mary sent in her resignation, sold her house and most of her furnishings, gathered her personal belongings and her dog, and drove home to Tarpley to live. Relatives and friends intimated that this new order of things might not be a bed of roses, some pointing out that "no house is big enough for two women," but Mama didn't spend any time worrying about that. She was confident she could get along with her own daughter. Besides, she wouldn't admit it to anyone but herself, but deep down she was tired of housekeeping and knew that if Mary wanted to take charge of the house she would be glad to let her.

Mary was not long at home before her bent for managing displayed itself. Her first acquisition was a dishwasher. Papa and Mama thought that it was an unnecessary expense, but they went along. Before they became adjusted to that change, Mary had decided they must get a home freezer, too. She turned a deaf ear to Papa's argument that the "Polar Pantry" was adequate for keeping their meats frozen and they could can fruits and vegetables as they always had. Mary had worked with food processing before, so when the freezer was installed in the basement she was able to show them many new tricks about freezing. Mama and Papa became more interested than they had expected to be.

Millie had not come home for the summer but had worked in a girls' camp in Vermont. She wrote that she wanted to come home for Thanksgiving and to bring someone with her. His name was Jim and she seemed to think that he was the answer to all her dreams.

Mary and Mama set right to work giving the house a thorough going over. They washed the curtains for the spare bedroom windows and Mary worked late at night in order to finish the hooked rug she was making for that room. Planning menus and cooking meals "ahead" also took much of their time.

On the day Millie and Jim were scheduled to arrive they had everything ready. Papa, Mama, and Mary had a light meal early "to stave off hunger" until the travelers should arrive, but night fell and Millie and Jim did not come. As they sat in the living room waiting, Papa began to speculate. He thought it likely they had had a puncture or some other car trouble. Mama thought they might have started later than they had intended—Millie was always a good one to be a little late. They sat, uneasily, watching the clock as the minutes ticked slowly by. Finally as midnight approached they decided they had better go to bed because there seemed nothing they could do until they received some message or some news of the couple's whereabouts.

However, no one was sleeping when the telephone rang, and Mary was the one who answered. The call was from a hospital in Lynchburg, Virginia. There had been a car wreck, a collision, and Millie was in the hospital there. She was in a state of shock and had cuts and bruises, but she was not listed in critical condition. When Mary asked about her companion, there was a long pause, and finally the voice said, "The driver of the car was killed instantly."

They decided Mary was the logical person to go to Virginia, so the next morning Papa had the car serviced and Mama fixed breakfast and packed a lunch. Papa suggested that Mary should take someone with her, but Mary rejected the idea. "I'll stay until I can bring Millie home, and if I take somebody along, that will be board and lodging to pay for two people instead of one. We can't afford it."

In a week's time Mary and Millie were back in Tarpley. Millie had a noticeable limp, an arm in a sling, a bandaged head, and a bruised face accented by a black eye. Although the homecoming was subdued, Millie felt the sincerity of their warm-hearted concern. Just being at home with people who loved her brought her unutterable comfort. She had been given a leave of absence from teaching until the new term in January.

The seclusion of her own room seemed to be what Millie wanted more than anything else on the first days after her arrival, so she was told to call for anything she needed and was left alone. Gradually, she seemed to become more like her old self and to want to be with the family. She began to help with the chores. When Mary decided it was time to put up the Christmas tree, Papa got the axe, put on his boots and muffler, and started out. "Wait, Papa," called Millie, "I want to go with you."

She bundled herself up and they trudged off together. It was an outing both of them would always remember—the brisk walk in the cold, the good long talk they had enjoyed, and "just the right size" cedar they found made the afternoon very special.

After supper that night Papa wanted to play a game of Rook, his current favorite. Mama and Mary played partners against Papa and Millie. Mama and Mary (who was the best player) won the first game, and since everybody knew that Papa wanted awfully to win, Mary suggested that they change partners. "Oh no," he said, "Millie and I are doing just fine. You just deal me a hand and we'll show them a thing or two, won't we, Millie?"

Mary and Mama won the next game, but for once Papa didn't seem to mind.

Day followed day and eventually the subdued holidays had gone by. Finally, Millie began to get her things together to go back to school. Mama came in to help and stood looking anxiously at her daughter.

"No, Mama, you aren't to worry about me," said Millie. "The accident seems ages ago, and I don't even feel like the same person I was. It was a ghastly way for a vacation to end. I'm glad I have no recollection of the crash. Losing Jim is terrible, but I don't think I could bear it if I had been conscious of his condition right after the accident or the ride in the ambulance or the clearing of the cars from the highway. But at last I've come to this conclusion. My students aren't responsible for what happened and I feel I must get back to them and try to make up for lost time. I remember a statement I read not long ago, 'Hearts break, my dear, but they go on beating just the same.' "

26

January was a month Mama liked. It seemed an in-between season of the year and a good time to go through the papers in her desk, re-arrange the cabinets in the kitchen, start to work again on her lone star quilt, or to crochet a little. Mama had given up knitting, since she was handicapped in that area. She was left-handed. Nobody seemed to mind much these days, but when she was a child it was the same thing as being cross-eyed or harelipped or clubfooted. One of the most humiliating experiences of her early school days was having the teacher tie her pencil to her right arm so she wouldn't try to write with her left hand. Mama still remembered how she felt when her schoolmates laughed at her. When it came to knitting, her being left-handed was a real problem. If she didn't use her right hand the patterns were all inside out, so she decided the world could get along without her knitting efforts. She had plenty of other kinds of handiwork to do.

Mary was asked to take charge of the Tarpley Public Library and accepted the job eagerly. Mama had felt all along that if Mary's health continued to improve she would want something besides the four walls of home to engage her attention. As soon as she began work in the library, Mary's enthusiasm for redoing the house was transferred to updating and re-arranging the library.

Since Papa was indoors a good part of the time in January, he kept the radio turned on incessantly. In fact, he so constantly sat in his easy chair listening to the radio that Mama told him he would grow to it if he didn't bestir himself and take a little exercise.

Most of the news on the radio had to do with the war. Mama had been stunned by the news of Pearl Harbor, of course, but for a long time the war seemed so remote, and she had so many troubles at home that the fighting didn't seem quite real. But when the news came that a local boy was missing in action and two more had been taken prisoners of war, when draftees were being called up on all sides, and when Tarpley enlisted men were being sent to camps all over the country, then the conflict became a dread reality.

The Barkers were personally affected, too. Danny was doing clerical work in Fort Belvoir, Virginia. Stan had just received a commission at Fort Gordon, Georgia, and he wrote Mama that he was now a "shavetail." Bob's oldest son had just been sent to Camp Roberts, California, and presumably was on his way overseas. Six months before she would have graduated from Stanford, Janet married a young lieutenant from the Midwest, both of them vowing she would go on to school until she was graduated. Susan and Greg's son was impatiently awaiting his birthday so he would be old enough to enlist.

The situation of the Barker family was duplicated by all their neighbors as it was by the whole country. Every eligible male was getting into uniform, and women's units were being activated, too. As Mama said, everybody was in active conflict except the old men who decided the country should go to war, directed its policies, and then sat behind a desk or in some sheltered place while others did the fighting. Most of the troops were young boys who didn't know what "expendable" meant and who were brainwashed with patriotism and fired by dreams of adventure. Mama had not forgotten the aftermath of the First World War.

She did think that people's attitudes were changing. During World War I a soldier kissed his sweetheart goodbye, prayerfully hoping to return to her. Now, it seemed that every draftee got himself a girl and married her before he left for combat. It almost seemed as if he thought that having a wife would be a sort of insurance to guarantee his return. Mama also noted that the great majority of these war brides were pregnant even before the soldiers left for foreign duty, and birth rate began to soar. She thought with concern about the future for this raft of helpless children coming into such an unsettled world.

The rationing of sugar, gas, and tires, as well as the shortage of other commodities, didn't bother the Barkers, who were glad to do without if it helped the war effort. But the problem of tending the truck gardening was a real worry. Papa could not get help, and neither he nor Mama had energy or strength enough to carry on as they had formerly done.

"Goodness me," thought Mama, "Papa is nearly eighty and here am I not far behind him. Did I think it was something that would never happen to us?"

Still and all, they managed. Greg found time to bring his tractor over and prepare a couple of acres for Papa to have a "victory garden," which, through Papa's patient efforts, yielded a surprising amount of produce. Mama, in turn, canned as much as she could.

One day, after a stint of canning tomatoes, Mama sat down to catch her breath. She said to Nella, who was visiting for the summer, "I declare, I'm developing bunions. Couldn't I surely have missed inheriting that?"

"Why Mama," said Nella, "just think, you have vegetable feet. The other day you said you had corns and today you say you have onions!"

"Yes, ma'am," laughed Mama as she tousled Nella's hair. "And I know a little girl who has a pumpkin for a head!"

Nella was very dear to her grandparents. Many of her little mannerisms were to them constant reminders of Janice, while her sunny disposition coupled with her gay chatter kept them amused and interested. Pete always paid the Barkers a visit when Nella was with them, and he and his daughter were the best of pals, but as time went on, it seemed that Nella considered Jane's house home base for her.

Early in October the message came that Bob, Jr., was reported missing in action. To the family it was practically the same as an announcement of his death, but Bob's wife Lula adamantly refused to believe her son was lost. She steadfastly maintained that she would hear from him again and insisted that he would likely be safer in prison than out with the troops. Nobody shared her optimism, but they didn't try to dissuade her.

Mama realized that nature being what it is, people can adjust themselves to anything, even to war. In Tarpley people reacted to the restrictions the war brought according to their own interpretations of what they owed their country in loyalty and to what extent they were willing to share. A black market and hoarders could be found, but there were loyal citizens, too, willing to make sacrifices.

For the most part, the inhabitants of the town went about their daily tasks as usual. The schools did not close, the shops stayed in business, the mills kept running, and farmers were busy. Over it all and through it all was a feeling of impermanence. All their thinking was geared to the theme, "when the war is over."

27

It was Mary's idea that a change of scene would be a tonic for them, so when Jane wrote inviting all of them to come down to Morgan Hill for a weekend visit to see their new house, Mary was delighted. They went, picking up Nate on the way.

"I thought the house you lived in was plenty good," Papa told Jane when they arrived at the new house. "This one looks pretty fancy for a Barker to be living in," he teased.

"Oh, Papa," Jane answered. "Don't you know you are the same person no matter what sort of house you live in?"

The big picture window, on the back side of the house where nobody could see it, and the private bath in every bedroom spelled luxury to Mama. She wondered what Jane and Boyd would do now that the children were gone.

Nella took enormous pride in showing off her very own room. "Look, Mama," she said. "I hope you like the curtains and the bedspread that are just alike. I picked them out all by myself. And the teddy bear on the bed is the one my daddy gave me last Christmas, and this badge on the dresser is the one we wear to Victory Club meetings."

At her grandmother's question, Nella went on to explain the club. All the children on Hillcrest Street belonged. The purpose of the club was "to help win the war." Each member had to have a victory garden and Nella had four tomato plants in hers. Meetings were held every other week and dues were five cents a month. A boy named Charles was president and Nella was secretary. She showed Mama the last entry in her book of minutes:

> The meeting met. We were at Jane's house. Charles didn't come and Mary decided in his place. We collected dues and played games. Then we ate strawberry ice cream and left.
> Nella Lavorini, Secretary

Soon Nella and Mama went downstairs to join the others. It was a real treat to have so much of the family together. Boyd played host in his ever cordial and attractive manner. It was no wonder he was so popular, beguiling anyone into forgiving his lapses and sympathizing with him. "A charmer if there ever was one," Mama thought.

They talked of family members involved in the war. Bob Jr. was still a prisoner and recently Joe Simmons was listed as missing somewhere in the Pacific theater, which made Susan's nerves as taut as a violin string. Janet would be coming home soon because her husband was being sent overseas, and Stan was a captain stationed now in Australia. Danny had shocked everybody by marrying an English girl a few months ago. Mama was uneasy and wondered if the bride would be able to adjust to life in America.

Driving home Nate said, "If I had had two hands, you know, I'd have been in World War I. There were thousands of veterans who couldn't adjust themselves to civilian life because they were wounded or shell-shocked or whatever. It will be worse this time since this war has lasted twice as long and so many more people have been involved."

On the way home they stopped by the post office to pick up the mail. Among the letters was a telegram, which Mary tore open. "Heavens to Betsy!" she exclaimed and sat down suddenly. Then she shook her head unbelievingly and said, "Well, I never! I n-e-v-e-r!"

She passed the telegram to Papa, who read aloud, "Married today in Little Church Around the Corner. Letter follows. Millie and Pete." Papa snorted and said, "Why, he's already her brother-in-law. That's some sort of incest, isn't it?"

Mama quickly put his mind at rest about that. "No, Papa," she said. "They really are no kin at all. If a man wants to marry his deceased wife's sister and the said sister is willing to have him, there's no law against it. But a little warning would have made the news a bit more palatable."

"Millie didn't have to marry Pete. What was the matter with that other fellow she was going with?" growled Papa.

"And just why are you so concerned about Millie?" Mary asked him. "Why don't you worry a little bit about me since I haven't ever been married?"

Papa's eyes twinkled as he answered her, "If you were to get married, I'd know you were going to be all right, but I would be a mite anxious for your husband!"

The summer was almost gone when V-J Day actually arrived and the war was officially ended. It changed the pattern of life for millions of people. While there were joyous homecomings for those whose loved ones came back alive and uninjured, there was also unutterable sadness for those whose sons had been lost in combat. The soldiers returning were not the same young men who had gone forth eagerly to defend their country. They were often disillusioned to discover that America was not the haven against all frustrations they had imagined while overseas. Thousands of war brides, many with young children, had lost their husbands to the war or had been abandoned by them. Confusion instead of peace seemed to be the outcome of the war.

At a Home Demonstration Club meeting that fall, an acquaintance sat next to Mama and said in a not-so-soft voice, "Cora, what has happened to the people in your church? Is it true that Jim Grey has run off with Tom Martin's wife and split up two families? And isn't he on your board of stewards? I don't suppose you could blame that on the war, could you?"

Mama's face turned red and she stammered a little. "I—I guess you'll have to ask someone better informed than me."

But the barb had gone home. Already embarrassed about the effect of the scandal on the church, Mama resented the implication that an affair like this was not likely to be found in her neighbor's church. Talking to Papa that night about the club meeting, Mama told him what Jessie Moser had said. His reply was, "A lot of things like that are happening these days. I don't know what has brought it about, but the standards people lived by have certainly undergone a change. But just you wait and see. One of these days some sort of upheaval will happen in Jessie's church, too. All the holier-than-thou people are not in one congregation."

His prediction was entirely correct. In a few months, the pastor of Jessie's church left his wife and three children for a girl half his age. Mama's urge was strong to say to Jessie, "Just what has happened in your church? Has the war had this effect on your congregation, too?"

In the next few months many changes took place. Bob Jr. arrived home apparently none the worse for his experience of having worked on a farm while in prison camp. Stan Brooks, now a lieutenant colonel, had decided to make a career of the army. His sister Janet, who had gone with her small daughter and husband to Montana to live, was already dreading the winter weather. Bob's oldest daughter was waiting to hear from a husband who seemed to be making no effort to communicate with her. Susan's son had been home and gone again. He was unsettled and admitted he didn't know what he wanted to do—a real war casualty.

Mama despondently wondered why people refused to learn anything from past experiences. In her lifetime she had had intimate knowledge of three great wars. The earliest and most vivid memories of her childhood centered around stories of the Civil War, of her father's four years in the Confererate army. She had heard the family speaking of its poverty, but she had never been hungry and her family had been no poorer than her neighbors. Her folks did not lose their home to the carpet-baggers, but they lived in it for years without being able to put a new coat of paint on the outside.

When World War I came along, Papa was too old to go, Nate was ineligible, and Bob too young, so her immediate family was ex- empt. But the war was very real to her since she had relatives and neighbors who were involved. She remembered the wave of lawlessness, rebellion, and wild carousing that followed the cessa- tion of the so-called "war to end all wars."

Who could have imagined that in less than twenty-five years the war machines would be geared to fighting again, this time involving all the principal countries of the world, using new and deadlier weapons, taking a ghastly toll of lives and property? The saddest thing about it all was that when the fighting did cease, the relief from ten- sion, the feeling of good will, and the sense of peace which everyone expected simply did not materialize. The only conclusion Mama could draw was that "a war is an instrument of destruction where even the winner loses."

28

One brisk morning in December, Nate, who had recently retired and returned to Tarpley to live, went to the post office and brought back a thick letter from Danny. That in itself was an event, for he was not a regular correspondent. The Barkers sat at their cozy kitchen table while Mary read the letter aloud. The letter brought the family up to date on his future plans, explaining that he and his wife Sheila had decided to make their home in England. He had found a job in a publishing house and Sheila would return to her pre-war position as a receptionist in a doctor's office. The real purpose of the letter, though, was to tell the family that they wanted to come to the States for a holiday before really settling down. He wanted Sheila to see where he had grown up and he hoped that other members of the family could come home for Christmas too so they could have a sort of "get acquainted" reunion.

Only that morning Mama had been thinking of the kind of Christmas they would have that year. She wouldn't have to worry about a large meal—she could just make dressing for one of Papa's hens, and the four home folks could enjoy a quiet, uneventful day. Somehow the idea especially appealed to Mama. "I must be getting old," she thought.

Even before Mary had finished reading Danny's letter, however, Mama had given up her ideas about a quiet Christmas and was making plans around the biggest turkey she could find. Of course they would tell Danny that they would try to do as he wished, and at once they began to count the number of guests they might have. Mary said to Papa, "At least Nate and I won't be adding any more family members to the crowd. Aren't you glad we're both old maids?"

"With thirty people in the family we'll have all we'll need." Papa conceded. "This is going to be worse than a shivaree."

"And I hope, Mary," said Mama, "that you don't start off with any wild ideas about turning out the whole house from cellar to attic to get ready for them. With that many people here nobody is apt to notice what the house looks like, and as for the cleaning, we'll need to do that after they've come and gone."

Although Christmas was four weeks away both Mary and Mama knew they would go all out to try to make the holiday special, so they began planning furiously for the homecoming. There were menus to concoct, sleeping arrangements to be worked out, and yule decorations to be made and hung. The dining table with its extensions would seat twelve people and the kitchen table would accommodate eight, but that made only twenty places. This problem was solved when a friend of Mary's offered a folding table which would seat eight. Since two of the guests were infants who could only use high chairs, this helped to make a place for everyone to sit down at the beginning of the meal. Susan would help with the baking and bring dishes and cutlery over to fill the gaps, as Mama said.

They began to hear from the children. Bob and Lula with all of their five children, the daughter-in-law, and the grandson would come; Pete, Millie, and Nella would get there for the weekend; Jane wrote that she and Boyd would be up for the day only, bringing Janet and her baby; Stan would fly down from Washington for the day also; and Danny and Sheila planned to arrive on Christmas Eve.

"Oh, I do wish Janet's husband could come," said Mary. "If only he were here that would make it one hundred percent—every last member of the family under one roof at the same time!"

"No, it wouldn't," said Mama. "Janice is missing."

A week before Christmas, Susan's boys brought bunches of holly and mistletoe from the Simmons farm along with a beautifully shaped six-foot native cedar tree, which was placed in front of the big windows in the living room. Long strings of popcorn were looped around it, and star-shaped cookies decorated the tips of the branches, but the new and special feature for the Barkers was the colored lights which Jane had sent them. Years ago Papa had turned thumbs down on real candles for the tree because of the risk of fire, so the electric bulbs were especially welcomed. On the mantel they arranged one of the ceramic manger scenes Mary had made for each of the households the year before.

Bob and his family arrived in two cars just before dusk on Christmas Eve, followed soon by Pete, Millie, and Nella. Danny and Sheila called to say that they were spending the night in Asheville and would see them before noon the following day. Counting the folks at home, that made sixteen people to be housed for the night. Mary was intent on placing a certain number in each of the four bedrooms, but some of the young folks brought their sleeping bags and scattered themselves all through the house.

Christmas morning dawned clear and cold, but since it was dry underfoot outdoor activities were in full swing. The old tennis court on the south side of the house was soon in action, while some of the youngsters set out to climb Hamburg Mountain with Greg as guide. Danny and Sheila wanted to look over the town and surrounding landscape, and some of the relatives went with them. Most of the women spent the morning in the kitchen, helping Mama, as Susan said, "to feed Coxey's Army."

They were busy every minute but by planning and working together the dinner was ready when it was expected. Each of the three tables had its own serving dishes, its own salad, pickle and relishes, its own bowls of rice, sweet potatoes, and green beans, and its own basket of homemade rolls. Papa was called into the kitchen to slice the turkey and ham. He did so and put some of each on three platters.

Danny came into the kitchen a few minutes before the meal started and drew Mama aside. "Mama, you know Sheila is English and on special occasions like this she expects to have wine served with the meal. Do you think Papa would object if we had a little of the wine we brought with us?"

"I think you already know what the answer will be, Danny, for you know how adamant your father is. When he has once convinced himself that a thing is right or wrong, nothing can change him. Don't you remember when Nate and Mary wanted to play bridge? Papa said they could play Rook, Flinch, Authors, dominoes, checkers—anything—but a game with a pack of cards that had a king, queen, and jack in them could never come in his house!" She stirred the rice vigorously for emphasis.

"I really don't think Sheila would mind," she went on. "She seems quite sensible and down-to-earth to me, and you could tell her we mountaineers are a pretty independent lot of folks and "set" in our ways. I have some good grape juice already cold and some blackberry acid—the kind you used to like— and I think that either of those will serve just as well."

"O.K., Old Lady, you win," said Danny with a grin.

When they were all seated, Papa returned thanks. Mama hoped he would add to his familiar blessing some little mention of their special pleasure in having the whole family with them, but he didn't.

Just as he repeated every day at dinner he said "Make us mindful of others as we partake of this food. Bless it to our use and us to thy service. Amen."

Little one-year-old Nancy was given grape juice in Danny's pewter baby cup. Expecting anything she drank to be milk, she took a sip of the juice, made a wry face, and immediately turned the cup upside down on the tray of the high chair. Janet rushed up with a towel to mop up the juice. Then she washed the mug and filled it with milk.

This little incident seemed to bring to mind a train of childhood reminiscences. Mary said, "Nate, do you remember the time you got baptized at the table with buttermilk?" To the rest of the listeners she explained, "The minister was having dinner with us that Sunday, and it so happened he had christened a child at the morning service. Nate, Jane, Bob, and I all sat on a long bench on one side of the table, and as the children were taught back then, we sat at the table until the adults were ready to leave. Jane was getting restless so she took up her glass of milk, leaned over Nate, and said, "I baptize you in the name of the Father and the Son and here you go!" And so saying she emptied the contents of her glass on Nate's head."

"Was that the end of the story?" asked Pete.

"Well, at least it was the end of the dinner party!"

"Susan, you tell about the time you and Millie got into the ants' nest,"said Jane.

"Not me," Susan replied, "if it's told let Millie do the telling."

That story was told, and another and another. The ones who had heard them before seemed to enjoy them more than ever. Eventually Boyd looked at his watch. "My friends," he said, "as pleasant as this is, we poor folks who have to work tomorrow need to be getting on with the tree and then starting our trip back home."

They trooped into the living room, the first to arrive taking possession of all the chairs and couches and the overflow sitting in a semicircle on the floor opposite the tree. Greg had agreed to act as Santa

Claus and Susan had fixed a costume for him. He said he'd wear the suit, pillow front and all, but he drew the line at putting on the beard. In thirty minutes Santa with some helpers had stripped the tree and removed the stacks of packages from the floor around it. Everyone tore open the packages the minute they were received, and as the happy recipients shouted thanks to pleased donors, the room became noisier and noisier. When things had calmed down a bit Mary said, "I know we can't spend much more time, but let's have a song or two before you leave."

With Danny and his banjo and Pete with his guitar, they all stood knee-deep in wrapping paper and sang "Silent Night" and "Joy to the World." After a few more carols they caught hands for a lusty rendition of "Auld Lang Syne."

The days following were a sort of kaleidoscope to Mama and Mary. By the time they got through with one meal and the washing up was finished, it was time to get the next meal ready. Friends and relatives dropped in to see those still visiting. In two days after Christmas the fruitcake was almost gone and Mary was in the kitchen frantically stirring up another one to insure that there was something to serve callers with their afternoon coffee or tea.

At last, on Saturday morning, the visitors began their trek back home. The house itself resembled a beehive as families tried to collect their belongings, pack their bags, and stow them in cars. Eventually the commotion was over, for everyone had gotten on his or her way. Papa announced that he was going to celebrate by taking a nap.

Mama was busy putting the house to rights, collecting the mountain of sheets and pillowcases she would have to wash, and pulling out the boxes for storing the Christmas decorations, when all of a sudden a paralyzing weariness overcame her. She sat down in an easy chair, thinking she would rest a bit before going on with her chores. It was sweet to sit still and know that she didn't have to hurry. It was ever so good to be alone and to sit there not even thinking.

Papa wakened from his nap, took a walk around the grounds, sawed a little wood, and stacked it in the shed joining the back porch, and then walked up to the mailbox to get the evening paper. In the meantime Mary had come back from a trip to town and had gone to the kitchen to see about supper. When they were ready to eat and Mama still had not stirred, Papa went in to see about her. "Cora," he said and shook her gently.

Mama opened her eyes, stared blindly ahead of her for a few seconds, and then asked foolishly, "Have I been asleep?"

When they had finished eating they still sat in the cozy corner of the kitchen, unwinding and living over the events of the last week. Mary was happy with the reunion and said so with enthusiasm. Papa said it was fine, of course, but something you couldn't repeat many times in a lifetime. Mama said she was like old Uncle Billy Bradford, who, when he was describing the departure of some lingering house guests, said, "When I saw the last car go down the driveway—them was the purtiest tail lights I ever did see!"

29

Spring came early to the Carolina mountains in 1947. Early in March Papa found a sheltered spot on the hillside dotted with bird's-foot violets. Despite his trouble in stooping, he picked himself a bouquet and took it home to Mama and Mary. When Mama had put the flowers in a vase and placed them on the breakfast room table, Mary said, "Wait a minute, Mama, you can't put those violets on that blue cloth—the two blues simply kill each other." So for lunch that day they had a fresh white cloth to complement the violet centerpiece.

That afternoon Susan came in excited to tell her news: Greg had agreed to sell the thirty acres of his farm adjoining the new highway. He had been reluctant to do so, knowing that if his father were alive, he would never have allowed it. But Susan had convinced him, pointing out that people must change as times change, that they had more land than they could tend anyway, and it would be so nice to have a little free cash for the first time in their lives. The times were a boon to Greg and Susan.

With the returning veterans establishing families, new houses were springing up everywhere. Builders described the new style as "functional"—long and low, glass-walled, and flat-roofed. Mama thought the homes looked sort of like a lead pencil.

In many ways it was a most unusual year. With the war over, it seemed a new life style was being adopted in America. Credit was easy. Young couples seemed to want to start with what their parents ended up with, borrowing freely for cars, appliances, and furniture. Even the government was piling up an ever increasing indebtedness each year, and the popular phrase to describe it was "deficit spending." To Mama that meant only one thing—spending money you didn't have—and she thought it would end in trouble.

Standards of behavior were changing, too. Mama knew she was old-fashioned, but the avalanche of divorce cases appalled her. She sorrowed bitterly over her first grandchild to get a divorce from her husband, and a few years later she was unreconciled to the situation when the granddaughter married again. "Thank God," she said to herself, "at least there were no children." But a short time later, Stan, who had had two children by his first marriage, brought his new bride

to see her. Mama couldn't understand how responsible human be-
ings could abandon their own children and justify themselves in their
action. But people were doing just that. Divorce was legal, accepted,
and becoming a way of life.

For one who had always considered herself an optimist, who firmly believed that the world was growing better, that the Christian
religion would one day be universally accepted, and that the precepts
of her Bible were standards that would never change, the world of
the '40's was a shattering revelation. But it wasn't just the world
around her that was changing. The conflicts and tensions of her own
emotions baffled her. She wondered what had become of her settled
views—the principles on which she had based her thinking and the
pattern of life she had tried to follow.

But changing or not, day followed day and the routine of their
lives went on. The ordinary household chores took longer and seemed more difficult to perform, so much so that she and Papa were both
"tuckered out" by noon and had to have a rest before they could do
any more work that day. They were ever so grateful for Greg's help
to Papa and for the days that Susan spent in Mama's hot kitchen,
even though she had the same sort of work to do in her own home.

One Sunday afternoon when the midday meal was over, Mary
announced that she and a friend were going to Asheville to attend
a lecture at the auditorium. Nate had gone to Atlanta for the weekend,
so Mama and Papa were by themselves. Mama settled herself to write
her regular weekly letters to the children. Papa said he felt sort of
drowsy and wanted to lie down. He took the Sunday paper with him
so he could read a little and then have a nap.

Mama was busy for a time with her correspondence. It was so
quiet that the clock's ticking sounded loud in the stillness. After a
while Mama leaned back in her chair and dropped off to sleep, too.
She awakened to the realization that the day was far gone and it was
about time for Mary and Nate to be coming home. She thought she
had better wake Papa up or he would never get to sleep later. She
went to the bedroom and called, "Are you going to sleep all day?"

There was no answer, so she opened the door and went in. She
was immediately conscious of an eerie stillness which sent a chill of
fear through her. She stood there unable to speak, unable to move,
staring at and seeing nothing. She was not even aware of Mary's coming into the room or of her taking her arm and leading her away.

In the kitchen Mary made a strong cup of tea and urged her mother to drink it. Little by little the numbness left her and she could accept the reality of what had happened. She laid her head on her arms on the table and sobbed softly. Soon Nate came in and was told the sad news. Mama said to him, "How in the world could it have happened like this? I was right in the house and didn't realize anything was wrong."

"But, Mama," said Nate, "think of what a beautiful way to go. He didn't suffer any pain for he lay quietly on the bed relaxed and peaceful. He simply went to sleep."

All the children came home to see their father laid to rest—even Danny and Sheila from London. The funeral was held in the little white church where the Barkers had worshipped ever since they had moved to Tarpley. The church was filled with relatives and friends of many years. "I wonder why they don't toll the bell like they used to?" a young boy asked. "When my grandpa died they tolled it once for every year of his age, and he was seventy-seven years old."

From the church the procession drove a few blocks to the cemetery, where the rites were concluded. As the crowd began to disperse, Mama thought it was somewhat like a reunion, for people who had not seen each other for a long time began to greet each other and renew acquaintances.

Mary and Nate, who stood on either side of their mother, asked her if she would like to leave. Slowly she shook her head back and forth and remained where she was. She stood silhouetted against the brilliant color of the autumn sunset, a plump little woman in a neat black dress. She knew the service was ended, but she was loath to leave her companion of more than fifty years.

30

The Barker household went on much as if there had been no interruption. Mama helped with the housekeeping and did her usual chores automatically, but she admitted to herself that she felt adrift with nothing to which she could cling. To fill the empty hours she worked harder than ever on her project to make a bedspread for her grandchildren. She had planned to make either a quilt or a crocheted afghan for each one of them. It was a big undertaking since she had so many grandchildren, but she thought she could at least do that for them to remember her by.

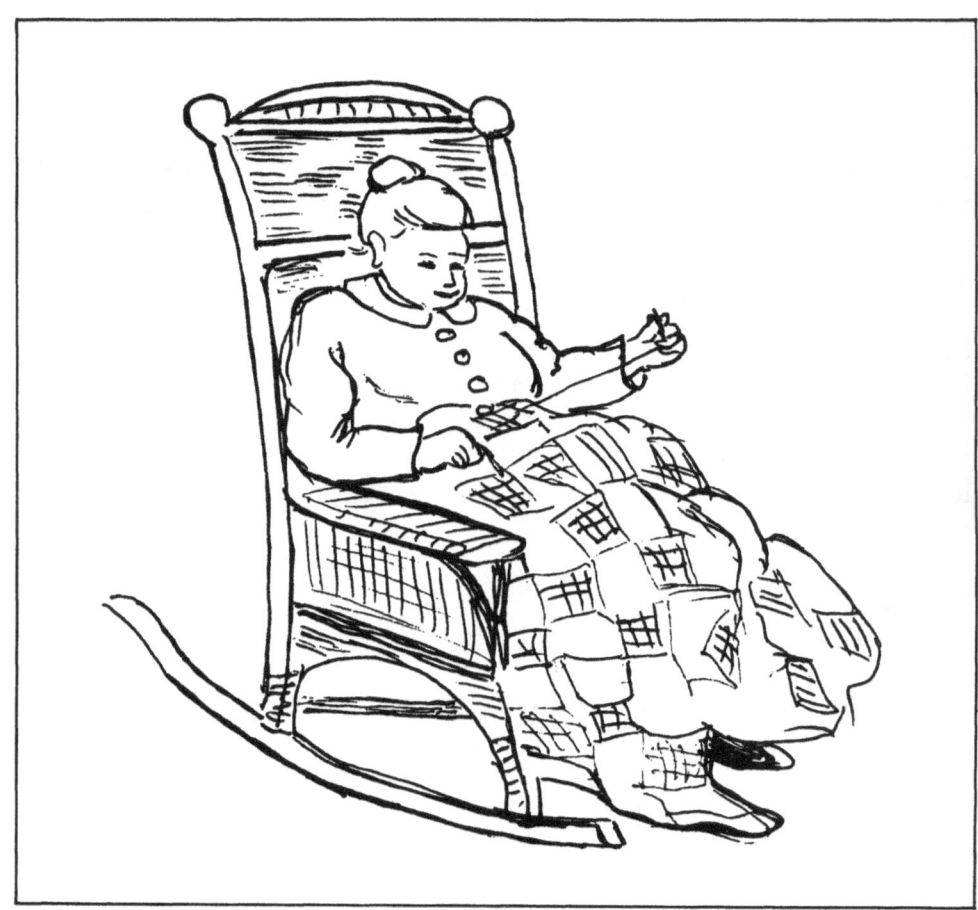

One day she received a telephone call from Jane. After they had exchanged family news, Jane said, "Mama, Boyd and I are going to Europe this summer and we want you to go with us. You and I can sail over on one of the Queens, and Boyd will fly over later to meet us."

"You surely can't be serious, Jane. You know I don't have the means to go gallivanting around in foreign countries. Besides, I don't know how to act."

When Mama left the phone that day she was sure that Jane understood how utterly impossible it would be for her to go to Europe, but in a few days Mama was shocked to find that she was planning to go to Europe with the Brooks. She hardly knew how it came about that all her objections and doubts left her, and she began looking forward with enthusiasm to visiting countries she had never dreamed of being able to see.

Jane sent her brochures from Bronson Tours. They gave instructions about places to be visited, the time to be spent at each, the sort of clothes to take along, and the amount of luggage each person would be allowed to carry. Mama's enthusiasm grew with her studying, and she applied herself conscientiously to getting out her history books and refreshing her memory about the countries she was to visit.

On the night before she left Tarpley, Mama began to have misgivings. She wondered why she wanted to go away for three months, separating herself by three thousand miles of water from all that was near and dear to her. But the next day she took hold of herself and decided that even though there was an element of risk in crossing the Atlantic, hundreds of people did so safely every week. Also, she didn't have any guarantee that if she stayed home she would be safe or that things wouldn't change in her familiar surroundings. So she finished her packing with determination, including in her prayers, "Lord, if it be Thy will, let us go safely on this voyage."

Her excitement was at a fevered pitch by the morning of her departure. Mary and Nate drove her that afternoon to Charlotte, where she spent the night with Jane. On the next day she and Jane took the "Southerner" to New York, where they spent the night in the Waldorf-Astoria. Jane said she chose that hotel to compensate Mama for their not being able to sail on the *Queen Elizabeth* or the *Queen Mary*. There was no space available on either of them, so they had booked passage on the *Franconia,* an Italian ship whose brochure made it look really elegant.

To Mama it was a once in a lifetime experience to stand at the pier from which *Franconia* was to sail and realize that she was one of the passengers herself. There were many small groups, and the majority of them were saying tearful goodbyes—evidently they were anticipating long separations. There was one rather loud party of cheerful well-wishers popping champagne corks, and on the other extreme there were travelers who acted bored with the proceedings as if an ocean voyage were a weekly occurrence and they saw no reason to make a to-do over it.

When at last the gangplank was pulled up, the huge ship inched away from the dock, with what seemed to be tiny tug boats accompanying it. Most of the passengers stood on deck to get a final glimpse of the Statue of Liberty, but soon the buffet lunch was announced, so Mama and Jane hurried along to the dining room.

It was nothing short of a feast, and no one was limited to anything. Boyd had told Mama they served such elaborate food because they knew lots of people would be sick and couldn't eat much, so they wanted to tempt their appetites. Mama, although she didn't know it then, was a good sailor and therefore did full justice to the food throughout the passage. She never stopped marveling at the quality and quantity of the food served.

She didn't have time to indulge in homesickness or uneasiness as the ship got underway. There was the getting settled in their cabin,

being assigned a table and time for meals, and a walk on the deck. It was unbelievable to her that going two laps around the deck was the same as walking a mile.

Mama decided the whole ship was like a small village uprooted and set afloat on the sea. They had all kinds of shops, a movie theater, a library, and a beauty parlor. For entertainment, there was a musical concert every afternoon. Every night there was bingo, bridge, and dancing. The management had devised activities in which all passengers could take part, and each day brought something different.

It was the ending of an era of ocean travel; however, no one would have believed the transition that was taking place, not even the ships' owners. If Mama had had an inkling that these floating palaces would soon be superceded by air travel, she would have been grieved because the five days she had spent crossing the Atlantic gave her a thrill she had never before experienced.

When the ship docked at Liverpool, a van was waiting for the Bronson group. They drove to Windemere to spend the night. There the group got a taste of how cold northern England could be even in the middle of the summer. The same burly Scotsman drove them the second day to the lake country of Scotland. Mama was petrified when they started out and she saw the cars coming toward them on the "wrong side" of the road! She closed her eyes in anticipation of a crash, but then she realized that the other drivers were also hugging the left side of the highway. "Mercy on us all," said Mama to herself. "What sort of country is this?"

On the drive through the lovely lake country of Scotland, they stopped at an inn which bordered Loch Lomond. Tea was served to them on the lawn, but Mama was so excited she could hardly drink her tea. The lines of the old song kept ringing in her ears:

But me and my true Love will never meet again

On the bonny, bonny banks of Loch Lomond.

As a girl singing that song, she had been saddened by the thought of true lovers never meeting again, and here she was an old woman now but seeing with her own eyes this beautiful scene. She felt romantic and young again, and she sorrowed for the young lovers of the whole universe who had the misfortune never to meet again.

Being a member of a touring group to Europe just after World War II was not designed for those who didn't have strong legs, good digestions, and plenty of pep. Mama thought she could keep up with the best of them, but there were times when she wished for just one day in which to relax and do nothing. She wished there were another boat trip spliced in with the tour! Mama never wanted anything she couldn't share, and she felt she must be on the alert every minute because she must take an account of these thrills back home with her and be able to tell them all to family and friends.

She had read about Edinburgh and the huge fortress on Castle Rock, but she was filled with awe when she saw the size of the massive structure rising perpendicularly above the street. How in the world did people get the material to build a castle like that? It looked so safe and solid, and the encyclopedia said it was over a thousand years old. She was also enamored by the flower clock on Princess Street. She had to stand before it a long time to check with her watch to see if the hands moved and if it was really keeping time.

31

After spending two days in Edinburgh, they went across England and took a boat over the North Sea to Holland. That trip was undertaken on a night so stormy that nearly everyone aboard was seasick and went without dinner. Even Mama had second thoughts about a boat trip being restful after that.

One thing Mama did religiously was to keep a diary of her travels. Each night she entered a complete account of what had taken place that day. She did it only to keep a record for herself, since she was convinced that if she tried to tell people about her trip in as much detail as she put in the diary, her listeners would be bored. Even with making a full account of her trip each day though, she knew she couldn't transmit the emotions she felt in actually being in places that had until recently seemed so remote.

In Belgium the director took the group to Aachen to visit an American cemetery. There were rows and rows of white headstones with names of United States soldiers on them. It was like an electric shock when Mama walked right up to a stone and read the inscription, "Lt. John Weston, Tarpley, N.C." John Weston had lived in the country as she did, and their homes were in sight of each other. It was almost like being present at his funeral, for he seemed very near and real to her. She stood there transfixed while her companions walked on without her.

Driving over a mountain road toward Baden-Baden, they travelled over a landscape dotted with little huts, used by the herders who looked after cows and sheep in the summer pastures. The driver, a self-confident young fellow, seemed anxious to exploit his skill, and in Mama's eyes he was going too fast for safety. She was nervous and kept closing her eyes whenever they rounded a curve. Suddenly a rude jolt made her eyes pop open. The bus had met a milk truck on one of the sharpest curves, and the bus driver was forced to go into a ditch to avoid a head-on collision. The bus lay on its side with the passengers scrambled "just like a carton of eggs," Jane said.

Everybody was jolted and frightened, but luckily none of the twenty-nine passengers was seriously hurt. Injuries consisted of bruises and abrasions, broken glasses, and loss of dignity. The bus was situated so that there was only one exit, the door next to the driver. Two men climbed on top of the bus and literally pulled the occupants out. Mama said it was like climbing out of a chimney. The experience was unsettling to say the least, but with only a few hours' delay the Bronson group resumed their schedule.

The next day they took a boat trip up the Rhine River, an excursion much more relaxing than the ill-fated bus trip. They were treated to the sights of acres and acres of neatly pruned grapevines and many picturesque old castles on the hills above the river. The volume of water that flowed up the channel amazed them, and the tourists agreed among themselves that it was quite romantic for the orchestra to play "Die Lorelei" as they sailed around Siren Rock.

Mail from home was terribly important to Mama, and she was thrilled because she got something at every mail stop they made. Many members of her family were thoughtful and wrote, but her ten-year-old granddaughter was the most faithful correspondent. At every mail stop Mama found a letter waiting for her from Jan, who would never know how much these letters lifted her grandmother's spirits. In fact, with every mail stop Mama realized how much she missed being at home. At first, the novelty of crossing the ocean and seeing countryside so different from the Carolina mountains kept Mama excited about the trip, but when there was a month left on the tour, Mama began to realize how footsore and weary she was becoming. She began almost unconsciously to count the days until she would start back home.

Boyd flew over and met them in Paris. He was his usual charming self and acted as if it were a privilege to escort Jane and Mama on sight-seeing expeditions. He took them to Notre Dame, the flea markets on the Left Bank, The Eiffel Tower, the Galleria Lafayette, Napoleon's Tomb, and the Arc de Triomphe. They had tea one afternoon served on the sidewalk of the Champs Elysée, which Mama enjoyed thoroughly. Boyd told her that he was saving the best for last, since he felt that a trip to Paris wouldn't be complete without an evening at the Folies Bergère.

At that stage of the trip, Mama would agree to anything that would help pass the time until she got home, so she started out in the best of spirits. Their seats were in the balcony, and it shocked Mama to see how practically everyone was smoking and throwing their cigarette butts on the carpeted floor. It made Mama nervous even before the show started, for she was afraid of fire and she wasn't at all sure that the cigarettes were thoroughly stamped out to be sure one wouldn't start a blaze.

Mama had heard of the Folies from some of her friends who had been to Paris, but she hadn't paid much attention to the description of them. She thought of it as just another event that "everyone" went to see. Sitting between Boyd and Jane, she waited expectantly for the show to begin. The first thing on the program was a rather clever monologue by someone inpersonating an Englishman. Then the chorus girls came on the stage. "My land," she said to herself, "they really are naked!" Each of the girls wore a big picture hat and a sequined traingle in a very strategic spot, but aside from that they were completely nude.

Of course, Mama disapproved and did not even find them attractive, but when she glanced over at Boyd she saw a big grin on his face. "That rascal would enjoy this sort of exhibition," thought Mama. However, she noticed that he seemed to be spending more of his time watching her than he was watching the show. Since he must be expecting her to be shocked and disapproving of the nakedness on stage, Mama resolved to do a little pretending herself. She laughed when anyone else laughed, clapped her hands enthusiastically, and acted as if the whole performance were for her special benefit.

Having tea at the sidewalk cafe after the show was over, Boyd said, "Just what did you think of all that bare flesh, Mama?"

"Well, with the weather like it is, I imagine those girls were more comfortable than we were up in that hot balcony," Mama replied.

From Paris the travelers returned to London and this visit furnished Mama the biggest thrill of the whole trek. Danny lived in a London suburb, so he met them and carried them to his home where Sheila and the twin grandsons were waiting to greet them. Their small home was attractive and well-kept. Like the proverbial English garden, theirs, pocket handkerchief in size, was in perfect condition. Not a weed was growing, not a branch of the shrubbery was out of place, and the little flower beds were riotous with color.

Mama was happy that Danny seemed so thoroughly acclimated and satisfied with his life in England, but she found it hard to realize that her youngest child, her little barefoot tousle-headed boy, who had grown up in the Carolina mountains, had become a virtual Englishman. He and Jane seemed to be so happy together and they had many things to recall about their childhood days. Mama wondered if Jane remembered her resentment when she discovered that Mama was to have another baby. Jane and Danny had had a special rapport all their lives, and though they lived thousands of miles apart, they were ever so happy to get together and could bridge the gap of distance or time whenever they met.

Mama thought of old Aunt Betsy's talks with her about her family. She remembered that she had said, "Dey ain' never really yours and all together 'cept when dey's little. When dey grown up, dey'll scatter and each'll go his own way. Don' think dey'll be what you want 'em to be neither—cause dey got to find dere own way."

From London they went across to Dublin and finished their tour with a three-day visit to Ireland. They were to take the ship at Cogbh for the return to America, but because of heavy rainstorms their last day, the *Franconia* could not come into the harbor and the passengers had to be carried out to the ship by tenders, and instead of a gangplank to walk on they had to climb a ladder. This strange procedure made Mama nervous, but she crept on board feeling thankful that at last they were on their way home.

She had a rude shock, however, for she expected the calm sea and smooth sailing they had experienced going over, when in reality this whole crossing was stormy and at times the winds reached almost hurricane force. There was dense fog at night, and the foghorn sounding sometimes every few seconds filled her with dread. The ship was tossed about by the heavy seas day and night. Walking on the deck was no longer a pleasant prominade but an ordeal to see if one could remain on one's feet. "How in the world could two crossings be so different?" Mama thought. She would be ever so glad, if and when they reached the land, that there would be no more water to cross.

32

When the *Franconia* arrived in New York, a whole day late, listing noticeably because the cargo had shifted during the rough crossing, the more than one thousand tourists all seemed glad to have that leg of their journey behind them. After they had gone through customs, checked in at Grand Central Station, and claimed their seats on the "Southerner," Mama thought she could never wait the night through so she could actually get home. When Nate and Mary met her at 6 a.m. at the station in Charlotte, she seemed to have lost the power of speech or of movement. She stood there trembling, overcome by her emotions. Although she couldn't communicate with them for a time, she said later she had never been so happy in her life before. She had been gone three months and had traveled thousands of miles, but she was home again and she found that no great calamity had befallen her family while she had been away. In fact, she wondered if they had even missed her very much while she was gone!

Since it was late August, there was canning and preserving to do, and she was soon back in the old routine of housekeeping and homemaking chores. One afternoon she went upstairs to lie down after clearing away the dinner dishes, and she thought about her trip. She certainly was grateful to Boyd and Jane for the trip, and she realized she would never be just the same woman she was before she went.

Studying history and reading about countries helped, but nothing compared to the actuality of visiting these places and seeing with one's own eyes foreign ways of life and being a part, if only for a few days, of daily living in a different country. The trip had helped her to see how little she knew about the globe she lived on. She had thought that the European trip would make her a "well-traveled" person, but what the wonderfully pleasant experience had brought home to her was that as far as becoming a traveler, she had only touched the tip of the iceberg. When she realized she had not set foot in South America or Africa, or countries such as Russia, China, India, and Japan, or goodness knows a whole world of other smaller countries she couldn't even name, she was appalled at her own ignorance. At least, she hoped she knew enough to realize her limitations, and she felt that she had learned things she had not expected to by going on her trip.

For one thing, she thought she understood Appalachia better than she ever had before. To outsiders it was considered a place where everybody was poverty stricken and where people couldn't help themselves. She had to admit there were some like that, but being a mountain woman "born and bred" she couldn't feel herself very different from the average run of people she met. It was like the old adage, "Give a dog a bad name and you just as well hang him." People who lived away from Appalachia had the impression that being from the mountains meant being underprivileged and on the poverty level. But Mama realized that other places come in for their share of being pinpointed by certain characteristics that are exploited by the press.

On the day that Mama had taken the trip up the Rhine, she had sat next to an English woman who had settled down for a long chat. She told Mama she was expecting to visit the United States next summer and seemed to want to discuss the proposed visit to get help in selecting the places she particularly wanted to see. Mama thought, "She'll be asking me about places I haven't seen myself." First the English woman had talked about New York, where the streets were like canyons because of the Empire State Building and other skyscrapers. She had heard also about the marvelous shopping centers and the supermarkets. Then she mentioned the Grand Canyon and Florida's sandy beaches. Mama wondered if the woman thought that America was the size of England.

"There's one place, though, that I would not care to visit," continued her companion. "Chicago would be off limits for me. I don't think I would feel safe in the vicinity of Al Capone and his gangsters."

Instinctively, Mama wanted to defend her country. "The press, you know, wants sensational news to catch the public eye, and sometimes one group or even one person's misdeeds can give a whole city a reputation that is unjustified and hard to live down. Chicago is indeed a prosperous, modern, and interesting place to visit, and it is the second largest city in America. You would be as safe there as anywhere else where millions of people are living in a congested area."

Her companion did not answer, and Mama was sure that her listener was unconvinced, but she had to try. It made her think of the Englishman and the American she heard arguing on the boat. The former was sure that the left side of the highway was the "right" one, and the American was just as positive that the right side was the only "right" one! After listening to them, Mama decided they really had no convincing arguments for either side—it was simply a matter of each person being loyal to a custom of his native land. And wasn't that feeling instinctive and universal?

No matter what the place of one's birth, be it mountain, desert, or plain, each individual has a love for and a sense of loyalty to that spot. Mama understood and shared that feeling herself. To her there was no place on earth quite like the Blue Ridge Mountains of her native Carolina. The great majority of the people there were simple, honest, pure Scotch-Irish descendants. They were hard-working, God-fearing, church-going folks who were ambitious for their children to have advantages that had been denied them. When all was said and done, most of these mountain folks were the salt of the earth, and she was proud of being one of them herself.

Mama remembered Aunt Betsy's advice to her about her children, that they would be hers only when they were little. Mama thought how right she had been. Her children had gone their separate ways and had chosen what they would do. She had children and grand-children scattered all over the United States and one family in England. In some cases she had hoped that they would follow a different course, but as Aunt Betsy had said, "You cain' do nothin' about it cause dey ain' gwine ask you."

Mama could not cope with the current attitude about families, with divorce so easy and the number of children in a family so small. She had grown up thinking that a woman's real mission in life was to have as many children as God willed and to give them advantages she herself had not had. Even though her children were scattered now, she still felt close to each of them, rejoicing with them when they were successful and sorrowing with them when they were in trouble. They had not all lived up to her expectations, but she was honest enough to admit that in some cases she had expected too much.

Mama's reverie was broken by Nate, who came up to her room with a letter from Jane. She read the note and said, "They want to come up for dinner and bring along Janet's little boy from Minnesota. We haven't seen him since he was a year old."

The letter seemed to rejuvenate Mama. It would be nice to have a chance to talk to Jane about the European trip they had shared, it would be fun to see Boyd, for he always livened things up, and she would be so glad to see the great grandson again.

She remembered that Mary would be gone until the weekend attending a library conference, and she thought of Sunday dinner. She knew what had to be done, she told herself, and she also knew who had to do it. Under those circumstances, she rose a little stiffly from her chair and started toward the kitchen, saying to Nate as she did so, "I'd better be up and at it."

ABOUT THE AUTHOR

KATE PICKENS DAY was born on February 20, 1894, in Weaverville, North Carolina. Day graduated from Weaver College in 1913, and went on to teach in various public schools for five years before her marriage to Ben T. Day in Easley, North Carolina. Among her many accomplishments Day established Easley's first Woman's Club, wrote a weekly column in the local newspaper, and kept the books for her husband's business. After her husband's death, Day published a private genealogy of the Pickens family. The result of this extensive genealogy was the fictional book, *Only When They're Little: The Story of an Appalachian Family*. Day passed away at ninety years of age in 1984.

www.ingramcontent.com/pod-product-compliance
Lightning Source LLC
Chambersburg PA
CBHW030337020726
47493CB00004B/1304